DESPAIR AND TRIUMPH

John Noble Thrillers
Book Three

David Mackenzie

SAPERE
BOOKS

DESPAIR AND TRIUMPH

Published by Sapere Books.

24 Trafalgar Road, Ilkley, LS29 8HH

saperebooks.com

ISBN: 978-0-85495-739-2

CHAPTER ONE

Takoradi, Gold Coast, Africa, September 1941

John Noble leaned out over the deck-rails, watching the busy port workers calling and gesticulating to each other as they secured his vessel. He was aboard a steamer that had just come into the port at Takoradi, on Africa's Gold Coast. It was the first stage of a journey John was making to Singapore, a journey that had started twelve days ago when he had embarked at Liverpool. En route, John had experienced mountainous seas and strong winds. He had been all right, but many of the passengers had been unwell. The voyage had seemed longer than twelve days, and he was feeling tired, but pleased to have completed the first leg of his long trip to Singapore. John had been posted there by the RAF to help with the set-up of Singapore's air defences, something that was required because of concerns about what the Japanese may be planning in Southeast Asia.

John had joined the RAF as a pilot in Britain, after being accepted as a Commonwealth entrant from New Zealand. That was back in October 1938. By the end of April 1939, he had completed his elementary and advanced training, earned his RAF Wings, and been posted to a fighter squadron. That squadron was re-equipping with Spitfires at the time. Following the outbreak of war in September that year, John had flown his Spitfire on a range of missions. Initially, there had been little engagement with the Luftwaffe, and the RAF pilots had described the period as *the phoney war*. That had quickly changed when German forces suddenly pushed west in

May 1940, confronting the troops of the British Expeditionary Force. As a consequence of the German advance, the British force had fallen back, towards the French coast. John and his squadron had been tasked with providing air cover against the large numbers of German aircraft attacking the British troops on the beaches at Dunkirk, as they were being evacuated back across the Channel to Britain.

The almost overwhelming demands of the Battle of Britain had followed, beginning a few weeks later, in July. John and his fellow fighter pilots had been required to fly and fight continuously, to meet the waves of inbound Luftwaffe aircraft. That battle had lasted four months, through to October 1940, and it was the most difficult time John had known as a pilot. Many in his squadron had not survived, and he had been shot down twice. The second time, he had come down in Occupied France, where German soldiers had determinedly hunted him. John had appreciated the courage and commitment of the members of the French Resistance who had helped him avoid capture. A covert night landing in a field by a Royal Air Force Lysander had seen John out of France and safely back in England within forty-eight hours.

Just recently, John had been summoned by his Commanding Officer, who had given him the news of his secondment to Singapore. Whitehall wanted to fortify British defensive capabilities to protect their interests in that part of the world, his CO had told him. There was a concern that the Japanese might be planning an attack, so they could plunder the natural resources of the area. The Royal Navy would strengthen its presence in Singapore, and the RAF was going to position some Hurricanes there to improve air defence. Because those aircraft would not reach Singapore for some time, the current RAF presence in Singapore was to be reinforced with several squadrons from the Australians and New Zealanders. They would be flying the Brewster Buffalo, pending the arrival of the Hurricanes.

However, those squadrons did not have any men experienced in air warfare, so the RAF had agreed to send some of its experienced fighter pilots to help them. John was to be one of those pilots and would join a New Zealand squadron based at Kallang airfield. As part of his secondment, he was promoted to Squadron Leader.

After his ship had been secured, John disembarked. He was met on the wharf by an airman, who took him to the local aerodrome, now a busy wartime base for the British, about five miles from the port.

'Welcome, Squadron Leader. I understand you are en route to Singapore?' the friendly local base commander asked John when he reported to him at RAF Takoradi headquarters.

'I am, although I'm unsure of my travel arrangements from here.'

'I can help with that. Twenty-four Hurricanes arrived at the port last week, shipped from England for delivery to squadrons in Egypt. Three of them have been assembled and tested, and are ready to go. You are to take one of them to the RAF station established at Hurghada, on the Red Sea coast. Starting from here, Takoradi, and crossing Africa to Hurghada, is the route Whitehall has chosen to deliver aircraft to Egypt. It's officially known as the West African Reinforcement Route. Most of the aircraft we require in the Egyptian theatre are going to be delivered via this route, hence its name.'

John was surprised by the news that he was to undertake a trans-Africa ferry flight. He had understood he would be travelling on to Cairo, but had not expected to be flying there himself, in a Hurricane. He was just thinking that it would be a daunting piece of navigation, when the base commander continued his briefing.

'It will take you five days to reach Egypt from here. Once you are there, you will be taken by transport aircraft, probably an Empire flying boat, from Cairo through to Singapore via the Middle East and India. That journey will involve another five days of travel, I understand.'

God, it's a long way from Liverpool to Singapore, John thought. He had already spent nearly two weeks on a steamer getting to Takoradi. Now he was facing a long and probably quite challenging delivery flight to Egypt, followed by another few days in a lumbering and noisy flying boat.

'I have been advised that the plan is to have you in Singapore by the end of the month. Any questions?'

'I'm not rated on the Hurricane, so I will need to spend some time on the manuals and talking to an instructor before taking one up.'

'Of course. I have allocated Flight Lieutenant Langford to help you with your Hurricane familiarisation. You start on that tomorrow, first thing in the morning. With your experience in the Spit, it shouldn't take you long to master the Hurricane. Command is keen the aircraft be in Egypt by the twenty-first of the month. As I said, it's a five-day trip from here to Hurghada, so you should be away from here by Wednesday.'

'Thank you. That means I need to have completed my familiarisation by the end of the day tomorrow. Hopefully the weather will cooperate.'

'The biggest risk likely to keep you out of the air in this part of the world is a thunderstorm. They are large, powerful, and dangerous to aviators, so we stay on the ground when they are about. But because they normally occur in the late afternoon, you should be finished by the time anything arrives, if in fact we get one tomorrow. I don't really see weather interfering with your timetable.'

'The storms ground all operations? Are they more than a relatively localised disturbance?'

'Absolutely, with significant and damaging gusts as they arrive. We always ensure our aircraft are securely tied down if there are storm warnings out, although local forecasting is not the best in Africa. The thunderstorms we get here can be substantially more severe than you may have encountered back in Britain, with rapid vertical development, so if you have the misfortune to meet one when you're airborne, never overfly or you risk being enveloped by the mushrooming cloud. Always go around a storm and ensure you avoid any build-up by no less than ten miles. Get too close and you risk being sucked into the maelstrom, to say nothing of the severe turbulence you will encounter if too close.'

John tried not to think about what such a violent thunderstorm would do to an aircraft in flight.

'Now, the mess orderly is expecting you, Squadron Leader. He will show you to your room. There are just the three Hurricanes going at this stage. Check in at the ops room when you're ready, and they will show you the route planned.'

'Thank you. Where do I find Flight Lieutenant Langford?'

'He will contact you in the mess this evening. All right, I must get on now. I trust you'll have a pleasant stay here and the ferry-flight goes well. Goodbye, Squadron Leader.'

As John made his way to the officers' mess, he thought about all he had heard. He was still coming to grips with the fact he would be flying a Hurricane from here to Egypt. It was a long flight over unfamiliar territory with the risk of nasty storms. He appreciated that he would need to stay sharp.

After settling into his allocated room in the mess, John decided to go down to the operations room to have a look at the route planned for his flight to Hurghada.

'Hello, I'm Squadron Leader Noble, one of the pilots taking the next Hurricanes due to go to Egypt,' John said to the young, fresh-faced man who met him as he entered the room bearing a large "FLIGHT OPERATIONS & PLANNING" sign on its door.

'Flying Officer Robert Earle, sir. I'm responsible for the planning of delivery flights.'

'Very good. Could you show me the route and associated information for the ferry I'm to make?'

Robert looked pleased to be asked about his work. He beamed as he led John to the large table on which there was a map of the African continent, with the route to be taken by the Hurricanes carefully marked out.

'This is the basic routing. Full route guidance detail is still being put together for you. It will contain aerodrome charts and facilities en route, together with details of local contacts and accommodation arrangements. You will be stopping for overnights in Kano, El Geneina, Khartoum, and Wadi Halfa. When you reach your destination, Hurghada, a Bristol Bombay will take you on to Cairo. That will involve a flight of about two hours.'

John leant over the map, tracing the route from start to finish with his finger. 'What's the rationale for stage lengths?' he asked.

'We aim to have delivery flights completed by the middle of the day, to reduce weather risk. Afternoon thunderstorms are common. Also, the officer commanding delivery flights has a policy of avoiding any one leg of more than three hours flight-time. Ferry tanks have been fitted to add more fuel, but we always plan these flights based on not using more than seventy per cent of total capacity. That's to ensure there is always a good reserve available in case you need to divert due to weather or some other issue.

'Day one will involve some four hours of flying, completed in two legs. The first leg, Takoradi to Lagos, is three hundred and eighty miles. The second, Lagos to Kano, is five hundred and sixty miles. Depending on winds aloft, that's about one hour forty and two hours thirty, respectively. For planning purposes, we allow two hours on the ground at Lagos for getting a weather update, and fuelling and maintenance — both for you and machine, sir. So, with pre-departure briefing and checks here, an intermediate stop at Lagos, and destination refuelling and tie-down at Kano, you should expect around seven hours' duty on day one, which dictates an early start to avoid the afternoon build-ups.'

Robert went on to describe days two and three. They were of a similar length, but days four and five were shorter — only one leg of approximately two hours each day.

'Why are there two days allocated for the Khartoum to Hurghada sector, Flying Officer?' asked John. 'Khartoum to Wadi Halfa is just over four hundred and fifty miles, as I read the scale, with Wadi Halfa to Hurghada being similar. That's only about four hours flying in total, which can be achieved in one day.'

'Yes, sir, correct, but there are controls on using Hurghada that have been imposed by military command in Egypt in recent days. Non-resident aircraft can only land at Hurghada prior to ten hundred hours local time. No-one has said anything, but in my opinion the tighter controls for comings and goings into Egypt signal something's up in the Western

Desert campaign. It's possible to apply for an exemption, but in the absence of any strong reason for arriving outside the promulgated window, we thought it easier just to stay overnight at Wadi Halfa. Then we fly in from there early the next morning.'

'All right, I understand. Could I have my route guide as soon as it's available? I want to spend some time studying the planned trip. The guides will have map strips?'

'Yes, sir. There will be a topographical chart cut to show the route, extending fifty miles on each side of your planned track.'

'Thank you, Flying Officer. I'm happy with that.'

Back in his room at the mess, John began looking through the Hurricane manual and handling notes he had been given. Speed limitations and power settings were not much different to the Spitfire. Happy with what he had read, he put down the notes and allowed himself to fall asleep.

The next morning, John was on the flight line early. His Hurricane familiarisation instructor, Flight Lieutenant David Langford, was already there waiting for him to arrive. David had contacted John the previous evening and they had arranged to meet at the aircraft at eight.

'Good morning, sir,' Langford said. 'This is the aircraft you will be delivering to Egypt.' Then, without further ado, he launched into his presentation. 'The good thing about the Hurricane, sir, is its stability in the air and on the ground. The wide undercarriage helps on the ground, and the thick wing section provides a stable platform in all but very rough air. The Hurricane is not as slick and fine as the Spitfire. Solid, stable, and dependable is how I would describe the aircraft. The systems are relatively standard for this class of machine, and speeds are not dissimilar to those you will know from your

Spitfire experience. My only comment is that the aircraft's weight and size mean it has a higher rate of descent in a power-off situation, so there's a need to be conscious of that, particularly when rounding out prior to touchdown, especially if you are slow and not carrying some power during the initial flare.'

'Yes, I saw that in the handling notes. I'm happy to take the aircraft up now,' John replied.

In the air, John found the Hurricane had no unexpected traits, and he had soon completed a range of exercises, including some aerodynamic stalls and steep turns. The aircraft was benign in the stall, even when fully developed with some power on. In a steep turn it was stable, sitting there at a constant rate of turn, with no tendency to wander from the chosen altitude. He could feel the controls were heavier than the Spitfire's, but not uncomfortably so. He agreed with what he had read and been told: the Hurricane was a stable aircraft, with few vices if flown competently.

John landed after spending almost two hours practising a wide range of manoeuvres, and he was feeling quite at home in the aircraft. He was ready for his extended flight across Central Africa.

CHAPTER TWO

The next day, John was seated in a small office in the administration block at RAF Takoradi, along with the two other pilots involved in delivering the three Hurricanes to Egypt. The smaller of the two, Liam Townsend, had already introduced himself to John. He was from Northern Ireland originally and still had a strong accent. Once they were settled, the second man, who was the officer leading the meeting, greeted them both.

'Good morning. I'm Group Captain David Weston, Officer Commanding ferry ops across Africa,' he said. 'I will be leading tomorrow's delivery flight. You've been asked to come in today so I can take you through what we might expect on our trip. I'll also talk about some of the logistical issues we may encounter.

'I've made two flights along the delivery route, so far: once while testing it during an earlier study of options for the delivery of reinforcement aircraft to Egypt, and once when leading the first aircraft to go up to Egypt via the new route. If the conditions are good and we don't encounter any tropical storms, or dust-storms, it's relatively straightforward, especially on our first day. As you may be aware, any thunderstorms tend to develop in the late afternoon, once the day's heated up a bit, so we reduce the risk of meeting one by completing our flying by no later than the early afternoon on each day. The trip involves five days of flying.

'Day one is along the coast to Lagos, where we refuel, and then we go on up to Kano. The terrain isn't particularly high anywhere along our track — all the way through to the Red

Sea, in fact — but much of the route is over remote areas. As we fly inland from Lagos, you will see the dense tree cover is gradually replaced by what is mostly low bush. Typical savannah country. On day two, from Kano, as far as Geneina, the surface conditions are mainly scrub, with a few partially cultivated areas, but also some large areas of just sand and rock. Day three, Geneina to Khartoum, is nothing but desert. It's the area where we must be most alert to the risk of dust-storms. They can reach up to three or four thousand feet above the surface. If we do encounter such a storm, we must cross it at a height sufficient to be able to glide clear in the event of an unexpected shut-down. Don't want to have anyone forced to enter the debris cloud due to losing height if there's a mechanical issue.'

John found himself wondering what it would be like if he was caught inside a storm like that. Zero visibility, no question, but would the air intake areas block, or would the engine itself be compromised by airborne debris getting in? Quite possibly, he thought.

'On day four,' Weston continued, 'Khartoum to Wadi Halfa, the surface remains arid, mostly rocks and sand. We generally follow the course of the Nile on this leg. Then our last day is Wadi Halfa to Hurghada. Navigation is not difficult on that leg, provided we have good visibility, which is the norm there. Our track will have the Red Sea visible in front of us not too long after take-off, and when we eventually reach the coast, we should be able to locate Hurghada without any difficulty.

'Dead-reckoning navigation is difficult over the early parts of the route away from the coast, given the relatively featureless terrain. Normally we would have a Blenheim to lead and help with navigation, as well as carrying a maintenance chap and our luggage, but there's none available for this trip, so we are going without that assistance. You will be given a duffel bag by the flight sergeant. It's not big, but it's pliable, so you will be able to push it into the small space behind your seat. You can get the kit you can't fit in the duffel bag when your case is brought up by the Blenheim next week.'

Damn, thought John, *I won't be there next week when my gear arrives. I'm off to Cairo for my flight to Singapore next day.*

'This is a newly established route, and we have been experiencing some logistical problems. One-hundred octane has become available recently. It's an improvement on the eighty-seven we've been using, but whether it's one hundred or eighty-seven, supply is still a bit hit-and-miss at some of our minor staging points. Shell has been working hard to fix the issue and I understand our fuel supply should be in place, in sufficient quantities, right along the route this time. The other issue is comms. We can transmit locally to each other in the air, but sharing information between widely spaced stations — the entire route is well over three and a half thousand miles — hasn't been working well. That's been especially important regarding weather detail. Signals are busy working to remedy the situation, but adequate communications are not yet in place, so we need to be cautious because there could be unknown weather conditions en route. My preference, if we encounter anything significantly adverse, is that we return to our last departure point. I'm not keen to push on to see if we can get through. If in doubt, turn-about sums up my Central Africa cross-country strategy regarding weather.

'Finally, gentlemen, your flying kit includes a survival pack — a bit of food, a bottle of water, and some basic first aid gear, including insect repellent. That's important to cope with the many biting insects you will encounter if you have the misfortune to come down in the bush. There will also be a

16

service revolver included, for your protection. You will be in the wild, literally, and there are some big carnivores prowling around out there.

'The plan is that we depart, after checking the weather, at o-eight-hundred tomorrow. Our first leg, along the coast to Lagos, has sufficient observation stations connected by telephone, and thus able to call in their weather, so I have no concerns about forecasts for that part of our flight. Once we head inland, we will be in more isolated areas, so we will have to make our best guess based on the isobaric chart information we will get from Cairo. That's provided, of course, that there is a working telephone available wherever we are. I apologise, gentlemen; it's less than satisfactory, but we are early operators on a route through remote and undeveloped territories. Not everything we need is yet in place, or it may not work as required.'

John pondered what Weston had told them. They were facing dead-reckoning navigation over featureless jungle or desert, while dodging unexpected severe weather. If forced down, they would be stuck in the middle of nowhere, being eaten by insects or something larger. *Challenging*, he decided.

'Any questions?'

No-one had any, so Weston ended the meeting on a slightly more encouraging note. 'All right, be at dispersal at o-seven-hundred tomorrow, ready to go after we review weather and complete pre-flight checks on the aircraft. I want to be airborne by o-eight-hundred. Despite everything not yet being in place along the route, the essentials are largely there, and I'm confident we will manage without too much difficulty. No enemy aircraft are thought to be in this area, nor anywhere along our route. Having said that, our Hurricanes will be fully armed. The expected absence of any enemy aircraft will no doubt be a pleasant change from the skies of Britain,' he said, smiling at John.

At o-eight-hundred the following morning, the three pilots started their engines. They had met an hour earlier and completed all their checks and planning. As anticipated, weather reports had come in from both Accra and Lagos, and no issues were indicated for their initial leg. Airborne from Takoradi and flying in a wide Vic formation, John followed Weston, flying on his port side. Liam followed on the starboard side. The three Hurricanes levelled at six thousand feet and followed the coastline east, towards Lagos. Looking down from his aircraft, John could see the wind was strong. There were whitecaps on the sea below, extending some miles out from the shore. The air was not turbulent, but John noted the flight was having to hold a heading offset of ten degrees to maintain track to Lagos, confirming the presence of the same strong wind here, at their altitude.

The flight along the coast to Lagos was uneventful. It took one hour forty-five minutes before the three Hurricanes were landing at the RAF station established on the outskirts of Lagos. After fifty minutes on the ground, they had been refuelled and were airborne again, this time heading northeast to Kano. Forty minutes into the leg, Weston called on the radio.

'Hurricane flight, this is leader. I see a large build-up ahead. Looks like a developing thunderstorm. I'm altering our heading to avoid it. Looks like thirty degrees to the right will work. Turning now.'

John and Liam dutifully banked right to follow the group captain's aircraft. A few minutes later, John could see that the new track would give them a sufficient margin to stay well clear of the building storm. It was occurring much earlier in the day than normally expected and was at least fifty miles wide. It looked like the cloud tops were well up already, probably at around thirty thousand feet at this stage. As he watched, he saw flashes of lightning, highlighted by their backdrop of dark, ragged cloud formations.

Soon they were past the storm and had resumed their original track. John experienced some moderate turbulence as he passed, even though he was several miles away from the storm.

They were about an hour from Kano when there was an urgent call from Weston.

'I've got an engine problem. Its running rough. Fuel pressure is down.'

John responded immediately. 'If you've just changed to a ferry tank, try going back to mains.'

'I had changed, so I tried that, but it didn't make a difference,' Weston replied, then a few seconds later he said, 'Engine has failed. I'm going down.'

John looked at the terrain below. Reasonably level and open ground, so far as he could see, with some scattered areas of trees and scrub. Plenty of clear spaces to land, he decided.

'Setting up for a forced landing,' Weston called as he descended. John and Liam circled him as he went down.

You've got to get this right, John was thinking as he watched the aircraft lining up for a touchdown on what appeared to be relatively flat ground between areas of trees and bush. *This is no place for a crash which injures you, Dave. There's no help available out here.*

John saw Weston had left his undercarriage up. A sensible precaution — a rough surface would risk a somersault if he got his main wheels caught in any unseen hole, or in vegetation.

The engineless Hurricane was descending through the last thirty or forty feet, but quite slowly. Then the aircraft touched down on its belly and skidded along the ground, through the low undergrowth.

'You all right?' John called on his radio as Weston's aircraft came to a halt in a cloud of dust.

'Yes, no damage to me,' came the response, much to the relief of John and Liam as they circled overhead. 'You have my position; I suggest you go on to Kano and organise a rescue party. They will have some ground transport, but I appreciate it will be tomorrow before they can reach me. It's a road trip of just over two hundred miles, and the roads themselves aren't great. At least I've got food and water.'

John did not like the thought of leaving Weston, with a ground party having to find him over the next day or so. 'I have an idea,' he called. 'Could you check your immediate area and assess it for a wheels-down landing?'

'What do you have in mind?' Weston asked.

'Flying Officer Townsend could squeeze you into his cockpit, if there's a suitable landing area he can get down on. It would be much better if it's possible to land and pick you up, rather than just leaving you to be found over the coming days.'

'Let me check.'

John saw Weston climb from his cockpit and begin walking around, looking at the surface conditions. After fifteen minutes, while John and Liam had continued flying overhead at a low power setting to reduce fuel consumption and to make it easier to stay close as they circled, Weston returned to his aircraft and called on the radio.

'Reasonably even surface about two hundred yards from me, and it extends some distance on an east/west axis. Light easterly blowing, maybe ten miles per hour, so the proposed area on which you could land is into wind. No obstructions or holes, so usable, I think.'

'Very good. We can't see it easily from the air. I suggest you stand at the approach end and adjacent to where you want Flying Officer Townsend to touch down. Stand on the left-hand side at the beginning of the strip you think can be used, and he will land next to where you are standing, on your right as he approaches. As you stand there, extend an arm out on each side of you, to indicate the general line of the strip you have surveyed.'

'Shall do,' was Weston's response. John saw him jump off the wing of his bellied Hurricane, where he had been standing to use the radio in the cockpit, and walk briskly to the point at which the chosen landing area began. Then he stood facing south, with his arms outstretched, pointing east and west, showing the alignment of the strip he had checked and chosen.

'See that, Liam?' John called.

'I do indeed,' he replied. 'I will position to the west for an approach into the wind he's reporting, and touch down in front of him, on his right as I come in.'

As John watched, Liam adjusted his flight path towards the west and began descending. When Liam was at what John thought to be about one thousand yards past where Weston was standing, he saw him turn back towards the planned landing area. John could see Liam was flying a low-speed approach. His nose attitude was higher than normal, and he had his flaps down. He was obviously carrying more power than usual for a landing approach. *Exactly how I would fly it*, John thought.

Liam judged it perfectly, touching down adjacent to Weston, and at a relatively slow speed. His Hurricane bounced and lurched over the uneven surface for about three hundred yards before turning and beginning to taxi back.

John was partway through another slow orbit overhead, when he spotted some movement in the long grass about eighty yards behind Weston. He turned back steeply to have another look. What he saw shocked him. Four large animals — lions, he thought — were moving stealthily through the grass towards the group captain. He called a warning on the radio.

'Liam, there are some lions stalking Dave. Hidden in the grass.'

'Damn, I'm nearly back to him. Twenty seconds' more taxiing. Hopefully they won't have a go at him before I get there.'

'I'll see if I can scare them off,' John said as he increased power and rolled back towards the creeping lions. Diving towards them, he wondered if the noise of his aircraft would cause them to scatter, but as he approached, they showed no sign of abandoning their hunt. *Only one thing I can do*, he decided.

On the ground, Weston had not noticed John's aircraft diving towards the area behind him, the sound of his Hurricane being lost in the engine noise from Liam's aircraft taxiing across the savannah. But he did hear John's guns open up, and as he looked around, startled, he saw the earth erupting as the ground fifty yards away from him was pounded by large-calibre fire. He jumped with shock, then John saw Liam's aircraft drawing up alongside him, the canopy sliding back.

Weston ran to Liam's aircraft, clambered up onto the wing, and eased himself down into the cockpit. With a sigh of relief, John stopped shooting and circled back up.

*

'Squadron Leader, I've thanked fellow pilots before for getting an attacker off my tail. But it's usually a hostile aircraft, not some hungry lions.'

'Happy to have been able to help, sir,' John replied. 'I'm pleased they were scared off with my first salvo. I didn't want to have to target them directly.'

The three pilots and two Hurricanes were all at RAF Kano, having completed the rest of their leg from Lagos without further incident. It had been crowded in the cockpit for Weston and Liam, but they had managed.

'Things are not fully set up here, but I've managed to get some cold beers delivered to the hut we have been allocated for our overnight stay, so it's my treat this evening, to say thank you. I'm much happier sitting here than I would be under a tree in the bush out there.'

'You're lucky one of your accompanying pilots was small enough to fit you into the cockpit with him,' John replied with a grin.

'No doubt about that. Thank you for the ride,' Weston said, nodding to Liam. 'Are you both happy to continue without me? You are virgins on this route, so if you want to wait a few days until the transit Blenheim comes through and have it lead you, that's fine.'

John and Liam looked at each other questioningly.

'The next sector, here to Maiduguri, is only three hundred and thirty miles,' John said. 'That's just over an hour's flying, so a well-held compass course should get us there safely. The following sector, to Geneina, is twice the distance, but there are some checkpoints we can use en route — the Batha River and Lake Fitri, for example — in what is otherwise generally featureless terrain. And from there, the remainder of the route looks relatively straightforward.'

'I agree,' said Liam.

'All right, if you're both happy, I'm happy. Enjoy your flights,' Weston approved.

CHAPTER THREE

The ferry flight went well over the following days. John and Liam located destination airfields without difficulty. Sometimes, when the aerodromes did loom up ahead after some hours of flight, they were left or right of the track the Hurricanes were flying, but John and Liam found they were never too far off course.

The last stop before their final destination, Hurghada, was Wadi Halfa, just short of the Egyptian border. Even though it was only a two-hour flight from Khartoum to Wadi Halfa, John was feeling stiff and cramped in his cockpit by the time they landed. Thinking some exercise would do him good, he set out for a short walk after parking his Hurricane. It was a very hot day, and he was soon sweating profusely. As he walked, John could see the difference water made in desert areas. The Nile flowed past Wadi Halfa, and consequently the village had numerous areas of green growth. There were several varieties of lush plants and fruit trees, oranges mostly, all in stark contrast to the arid, brown terrain away from the river. After thirty minutes of slow walking in the heat, John was back at the airfield, his shirt wet with perspiration.

'Squadron Leader, Flying Officer Townsend is looking for you.'

John looked up and saw the gate sentry was calling out to him.

'He's with your aircraft, sir,' the sentry continued.

John waved to show he had heard and made his way over to the area where the two Hurricanes had been parked. As he got closer, he saw Liam standing next to a pile of stakes and ropes. He had a long-handled axe in his hands.

'Are you looking for me, Flying Officer?' John asked.

'Yes, sir. Duty Officer has just told me there's a sandstorm coming. No spare hangar space, so we need to secure the aircraft outside,' Liam explained.

'A sandstorm, or a dust-storm?'

John had been told about the storms in detail while chatting to a local officer over a couple of ice-cold beers in the officers' mess at Khartoum aerodrome the previous evening. John had mentioned that if they met a sandstorm, the plan was to be a minimum of five or six thousand feet above the ground to ensure they stayed clear of the airborne debris. However, the officer had told him that he would not need to be at that height if he encountered a sandstorm, as sand generally did not rise more than fifteen hundred feet above the surface. While sand was very abrasive, it was too heavy to be carried a long way up by the wind. Dust-storms, on the other hand, were made up of lighter wind-blown material that would go up to about four thousand feet.

John had listened in dismay as the officer had described an aircraft that had been caught as it had been taxiing after landing the previous month. A particularly ferocious sandstorm had come through with little warning. As well as choking every port and recess of the aircraft with its sand, it had abraded the front windscreen so badly that the pilots could no longer see through it. John shuddered to think what a storm like that would do to an aircraft caught in the air.

In answer to John's question, Liam said, 'A sandstorm was how it was described to me, rather than dust-storm. Does that affect anything?'

'Yes, it does,' John said. 'The chap at Khartoum told me the sand is heavier and will do more damage to an aircraft than the lighter dust. So, special precautions, I think. Which direction is the storm approaching from, do you know?'

'From the north, and it's expected to hit in about twenty minutes.'

'Right, let's move these aircraft behind that hangar over there,' John responded, pointing to a large building nearby, constructed from sheets of corrugated iron. 'We'll park on its south side for shelter, and picket them there. I see you have the stakes and rope already. We need to sort out some protection for the vital areas, as well, pitot heads and engine openings.'

The two Hurricanes were quickly started with the assistance of a couple of local ground crew and taxied into a position to park on the south side of the hangar. They were parked as close as possible to it, for maximum protection from the approaching storm. Both pilots were soon busy with the large axe, banging the stakes into the ground under the wings and tail of each aircraft. Ropes from those stakes to various tie-down points on the aircraft would help ensure the wind did not move the Hurricanes. They were parked with brakes set and control surfaces locked, but because they could still be lifted by strong gusts, tie-downs were necessary as well, even when sheltered behind the hangar. John kicked some chocks into place behind and in front of each of the main wheels.

'See if you can find some rags we can secure over the pitots,' John called. Because the pitots measured airspeed, he knew they would be hopelessly inaccurate if contaminated with sand grains, so covering them was essential. 'I will get some sheets or towels to stuff into the cowling intakes, so we don't get sand through the engine bay.'

Working fast, Liam and John finished securing the Hurricanes as best they could against the approaching sandstorm in no more than fifteen minutes. Then they quickly moved to the temporary building that served as the base administration centre, next to a row of small huts. The huts were for officer accommodation. RAF Wadi Halfa was sufficient to meet basic needs, nothing more. It would be improved in due course, but at present, apart from the station at Khartoum, the Royal Air Force had not yet fully established itself at the aerodromes it used along the Central African reinforcement route. The development of facilities at the various staging points was still a work-in-progress.

As John and Liam entered the aerodrome's main office, those already inside were clustered at a large window, looking along the runway towards the north.

'Here it comes,' said an older, completely bald man, whose only hair was what looked like grey fuzz around the back of his neck and above his ears. He was clearly one of the administrators at the base — too old to be an active duties member of the service, John decided.

John looked through the window to see what was being referred to. There was a billowing wall of thick, brown cloud rolling towards the aerodrome. It reminded him of a surf wave approaching a beach. The cloud churned and rolled rapidly over the ground, enveloping everything in its path. Its top looked to be about one thousand feet high. Then the storm hit the building they were in. There was a huge roar — the sound of millions of hard particles being blasted against the building by the strong wind. It went dark as the sand blocked out the sunlight.

'Christ, it's a goodie!' the bald man called. He sounded almost gleeful.

The force of the storm's front must be strongest as it arrives, John thought. It had hit with a bang, but now, after about a minute, he could detect it was subsiding. The buffeting of the wind was lessening, and the room was getting lighter. The noise of the sand against the windows and on the tin roof was reducing as well.

After the storm had passed, which took only another ten minutes, John and Liam made their way back to where they had parked the two aircraft, in the lee of the large hangar. John was pleased to see they had not moved, despite the strong gusts. A sheet of corrugated iron had detached from the hangar and had obviously blown some distance at considerable speed. It had embedded itself in the wooden wall of a shed, sixty yards away.

Covers were taken off the pitot tubes. They were secure, so had done their job and prevented sand getting in. The oil-stained sheets John had found in an adjacent workshop were taken out of the cowling areas they had been blocking. There was no sign of sand on, around or inside the engine.

'Looks like the aircraft survived that with no damage or contamination,' John said, smiling.

The next morning, John and Liam were airborne not long after first light. They were heading for the aerodrome at Hurghada, near the southern end of the Gulf of Suez, on the west coast of the Red Sea. It was an easy enough trip in fine weather. The Nile was there to guide them, and the Red Sea was soon in view from their cruising height of nine thousand feet. An hour and forty minutes later, the two Hurricanes were touching down on the base at Hurghada. It was a busy place. The Royal Air Force was working quickly to set the aerodrome up as the receiving point for aircraft delivered to Egypt to assist with the desert campaign raging along the North African coast.

Within an hour of landing, John was making his way out to the large, ungainly-looking transport aircraft that would take him to Cairo. A smiling young flight lieutenant greeted him as he approached the aircraft.

'Good morning, sir. I'm Flight Lieutenant Adams — I'll be flying you to Cairo.'

John acknowledged the flight lieutenant with a smile and asked about the expected arrival time in Cairo.

'It's about two hours fifteen in the Bombay, and we are flight-planned to be airborne in fifty minutes, at eleven hundred hours. We are exempt from the aerodrome traffic restrictions that cut in at ten hundred hours. I estimate our arrival in Cairo to be at about thirteen-twenty, sir. We're not fast, I'm afraid. One hundred and sixty cruise speed.'

'Thank you, Flight Lieutenant.'

'There are three other passengers. LRDG, I understand,' the Bombay pilot continued. 'They haven't turned up yet, but hopefully they will show soon.'

John was familiar with the emerging reputation of the Long Range Desert Group. It had been established as a reconnaissance and raiding unit. He knew many members of the small force were New Zealanders, experts in covert patrols behind enemy lines and efficient in combat, as some Germans, and the occasional Italian, had the misfortune to discover.

It was another ninety minutes before the other passengers showed up. They had been delayed somewhere and were apologetic as they climbed aboard the Bristol Bombay.

'Pleased to meet some Kiwis,' John said, already forgiving their lateness, when their officer in charge, Captain Bill Dunn, had introduced himself and his two lieutenants. John understood how timetable disruption could easily occur in a war zone. 'I've been hearing stories about what LRDG has been up to behind enemy lines in the Western Desert.'

'Ah, mate, you shouldn't believe everything you hear. We're just lurking around in the desert, checking on Herr Rommel's activities and doing bits and pieces here and there.'

John knew that was a massive understatement as to the intensity and success of the Group's operations, all at a time when the principal Allied forces had been pushed out of Libya, back into Egypt. The exception had been the defenders of the port at Tobruk, who were under siege by the Germans.

'I know you operate clandestine missions, so I won't ask you about that. I will just say good for you!'

'Thanks, mate,' Bill replied. 'I'm from Napier. You?'

'Off a farm in the Clutha Valley in Otago.'

'Ah, I know the Otago province well,' Bill responded. 'These two,' he went on, nodding towards his lieutenants, 'are from Dunedin and Gore, respectively, not far from you.'

'Harnesses buckled, please,' came the call from the cockpit. 'We are about to start engines.'

The cabin of the Bombay had a bench down each side of it. Not the most comfortable seat, and John had never liked sitting sideways to the direction of flight, but there was not much he could do about it. Once underway, the aircraft engines were so noisy that normal speech was not easy. After a few minutes of shouted conversation, John and the three members of the Long Range Desert Group gave up trying to talk to each other.

Just over two hours later, the Bristol Bombay touched down at the airport in Cairo used by the Royal Air Force. The landing was firm, not helped by the long, fixed, and rigid undercarriage legs that extended down from the bottom of the engine cowlings on the aircraft's high wing. John said a quick goodbye to his new friends from the desert campaign and set off to look for the officer in charge of the flights connecting to Singapore.

'How do you do, Squadron Leader?' said the officer who ran the transit services operating from the RAF base in Cairo. He greeted John with a firm handshake. 'I trust you had a good trip.'

The aerodrome was in the northeast of the city of Cairo, an area known as Heliopolis. The Royal Air Force had taken it over some years previously, but parts of the administrative facilities remained incomplete, as John could see. The transit service was not in an office. Instead, it occupied a small open area, with two desks and a filing cabinet, halfway down what was once a large aircraft hangar.

'The CO wants to see you before you leave,' the officer went on, without waiting for John's response. 'He is Air Commodore Ian McCarroll and he wants to brief you on matters relevant to the operation you will be commanding at RAF Kallang, when you get to Singapore. I will take you there now, otherwise you may miss him. He'll be off shortly, and you'll be too pushed for time to be able to see him in the morning, before you fly out. Is that all right?'

'Certainly,' John replied, falling into step behind the busy flight lieutenant, who was already striding off towards his CO's office.

Once they had knocked on the door and been invited to enter, they stepped inside to find the CO behind his desk.

'Welcome, Squadron Leader Noble. I trust the flights from Takoradi went well?' a smiling Air Commodore McCarroll asked. His rank and position meant he qualified for a proper office, rather than a more basic space in a hangar.

'Thank you, sir. All went well, in the main,' John replied.

'I understand you are out on the Empire first thing tomorrow, bound for Singapore, eventually. It's a long way. Five days of flying.'

'So I understand, sir,' said John with a nod. Then, after a brief pause, he went on, 'You had some information for me about the squadron I will be commanding in Singapore?'

'I do. Signal from Fighter Command in Britain. The nub of it is that the Hurricanes intended for you in Singapore have been diverted to Egypt. You will have to make do with the squadron's existing Buffalo aircraft in the meantime.'

John was dismayed. He knew the Buffalo was not an adequate match for Japanese fighters if hostilities began in Southeast Asia. 'That's quite different from what I was told as I was leaving the UK,' he responded. 'The message I had was that the Hurricanes were being shipped from Britain directly to Singapore, to be there by the end of the month. Why the change, sir?'

'It's because things haven't been going so well in the Western Desert campaign, I'm afraid. Rommel is making life difficult, so the orders from the top are that all available fighter aircraft are to be put into Egypt at this time. You will get your Hurricanes, but not as soon as was originally planned. Probably late November.'

'Well, I hope Command understands the inadequacy of air defence in Singapore based on Buffalos.' John wondered if he sounded petulant, but he thought it important to make the point.

'Look, I understand your concern,' McCarroll acknowledged, 'but those are the orders. The assessment is that the Hurricanes are currently needed more urgently in North Africa than in Singapore. The Germans are here now. The Japanese forces are still at home, with no military movements known, apart from their recent foray into French Indochina, and, of course, their existing war with China. Singapore isn't considered to be under any threat at present. Anyway, even if the Japanese do crank up some military activity further south than Indochina, they are not expected to try to take us on in Singapore, or in Malaya, for that matter.'

John said nothing, but he was worried. He knew getting technical and outlining the differences in performance and capability between the Buffalo and a Zero was a waste of time here. There was nothing McCarroll could do, even if he agreed that John's squadron was going to be in a difficult position.

Command was taking a gamble, hoping that Japan would yield under international pressure, pull out of French Indochina, and end its war against the Chinese. But if Japan did not take that course, the alternative could be that the army would move south, against the Philippines, Dutch East Indies, and maybe Malaya, to access oil and protect that supply once seized. Then Singapore would be in play.

'Very well, sir, I understand the reason for the delay,' John said after some thought. 'I just ask you to confirm in a signal to Command that in my view, the adequate air defence of Singapore is threatened by the absence of Hurricanes should there be any development in the area involving Japanese forces.'

'I can say that, Squadron Leader, and I'm happy to do so, but you need to understand the existing war priority. We are pressed in Libya. The Japanese are muttering, but there's no indication they will declare war on us, so that's the basis for Singapore having to wait. I suggest you return to OC transits and finalise your travel arrangements for tomorrow. Nice to meet you. All the best in Singapore.' With that, John's meeting with Air Commodore McCarroll was over.

CHAPTER FOUR

The Empire flying boat touched down on the sea channel adjacent to the aerodrome at RAF Seletar, Singapore. The channel was over a mile wide and had a useful northwest/southeast orientation, very suited to the prevailing winds. It was the principal place used as the alighting area for flying boats in Singapore, although the Kallang Basin, as the locals called it, on the southern side of the island, was also used from time to time. The chop on the water caused a few initial bumps and bounces for the aircraft until it slowed and settled its hull deeper into the water. John was pleased to have finally arrived in Singapore. It was thirteen hours since his aircraft had taken off from Rangoon earlier that day: ten hours in the air and three hours for refuelling stops at Bangkok and Penang. The day had been horribly long, and it was just one of five similar days he had been required to endure since leaving Cairo.

As a passenger, John had found the trip from Cairo long and boring, and sometimes rough. They had encountered numerous weather build-ups, particularly over the Bay of Bengal, and again over Thailand. The captain and his copilot had competently avoided the worst conditions by doglegging around them. Nevertheless, it was still not pleasant for someone sitting in the back of a lumbering flying boat, unsure what may be ahead as the flight crew picked their way around the cumulonimbus clouds growing into yet another tropical storm.

As he stepped from the aircraft, John was struck by the heat and humidity. It was still uncomfortably hot, despite the fact that the sun was setting. He knew that in this part of the world, it would soon be dark. There were no extended periods of twilight in the tropics.

'Squadron Leader Noble?' a voice enquired.

John turned to see he was being addressed by a young man in a khaki uniform. He looked at him closely in the rapidly fading light.

'Flying Officer Owen Gilks, sir, Forty-Eight Squadron, Royal New Zealand Air Force,' the man introduced himself. 'I'm here to take you to our base at Kallang aerodrome.' He gestured towards a jeep parked nearby.

As they drove to Kallang, John asked Owen about the squadron. 'How long has the squadron been here?'

'Only three weeks, sir, and we are not yet at full muster. Another three pilots are due at the end of the week. They had to complete some specific air warfare training at New Zealand's main training base at Ohakea before coming out here. When they arrive, we will have a full complement.'

'I understand the squadron has Buffalos at present, while you are awaiting Hurricanes?'

'Yes, sir, we have fourteen Brewster Buffalos, although some aren't airworthy at the moment, and there are some performance issues with those we have got flying. I hadn't heard anything about receiving Hurricanes to replace them.'

'What are the issues with the Buffalos?'

'Well, if I may speak openly, they handle quite nicely in normal flight, but not so in extreme manoeuvres. When the aircraft is loaded up, it can be unstable in certain scenarios, spinning is not approved, and it's difficult to loop tidily because of its sluggish performance and poor response to control inputs. There's plenty of room in the cockpit, and visibility is outstanding, but overall, it performs like a dog. It has nil high-altitude performance, and we have been having fuel starvation issues at heights above sixteen thousand. Full-power climbs usually result in engines overheating, forcing a power reduction and climb cessation. We just can't get to altitude on some occasions. Maintenance is a nightmare as well. For every flight hour, we are averaging two and a half hours of maintenance.'

'That's not a pretty picture you paint,' John responded.

They continued their journey to Kallang in silence as John pondered how they would cope while awaiting better fighter aircraft. As the jeep weaved its way through the crowded streets, alive with shopkeepers and street hawkers rather than traffic, John took in the hustle and bustle of people going about their daily lives. He recognised the devasting impact there would be on these people if the Japanese decided to attack Singapore.

That night John showered and changed into some spare kit he had managed to borrow, given his own gear still had to make its way to Singapore from Takoradi. He then made his way to the officers' mess to meet some of his fellow officers.

'Welcome to Singapore, sir,' said a man in the uniform of a flight lieutenant, who had moved across the room to intercept John as he came in.

'Thank you, Flight Lieutenant,' John replied.

'Richard Stark, sir. I'm your second-in-command. Let me introduce you to some of the others,' he said, turning towards a group of pilots standing nearby. 'Flying Officers Trevor Roberts, Don Salt, and Jock Gilbert. Gentlemen, this is our new CO, on secondment from the RAF, Squadron Leader John Noble.'

There were murmured greetings as they all shook hands with John.

'I understand you are all recently off advanced training in New Zealand, and this will be your first operational assignment?' John enquired.

'That's correct,' Don Salt responded. 'We understand we have some work to do to get ourselves fully up to speed in aerial combat techniques.'

'Do you have much time on the Buffalo?' John asked the group.

Don spoke again. 'I have thirty hours, sir. I've been through the flying instructor's course on the machine. None of the others, apart from Flight Lieutenant Stark who is also a qualified Buffalo instructor, has any more than ten or fifteen hours on the aircraft.'

'I will be arranging some air exercises to build squadron capability,' John said, 'but the first thing I have to do is get myself familiar with flying the Buffalo. It's a new aircraft to me.'

Over dinner, John got to know some of the pilots better. Richard Stark was from Invercargill, New Zealand's southernmost city. He had joined the Royal New Zealand Air Force at the outbreak of war, but his flying experience was limited to Tiger Moths, in which he had learnt to fly, followed by Harvards for his advanced flying training, and recently, the Buffalo. He had been signed off as a flight instructor on the Buffalo just last week, after taking a course run by the Royal Air Force at its base at Kluang, in Johor.

The others, apart from Don Salt, were more recent joiners. Trevor Roberts, a man of about thirty, John guessed, was from Ashburton, a small town in Mid Canterbury on the South Island of New Zealand. He was a keen climber and told John he had spent a lot of his time in the Southern Alps, a mountain range easily accessed from his hometown.

'I'm not married. Always too busy, out clambering in the mountains,' he told John.

Don Salt and Jock Gilbert were both from Auckland. Don was a keen sailor. He told John how he loved sailing on Auckland Harbour and the Hauraki Gulf in his family's yacht, and how much he was missing that now. He had spent a week happily sailing there, just prior to coming out to Singapore to take up his posting to 48 Squadron.

Jock Gilbert told John he had been in his first year studying medicine when war had broken out. He had decided he would put his medical career on hold and contribute to the war effort by joining the RNZAF. He was newly married, and while happy to be doing his bit, he made it clear he was missing his wife and his former life.

These fellows all seem to be nice chaps, John decided. He knew he would enjoy flying with them, but he also recognised the responsibility he had to keep them, and the other pilots he was yet to meet, as safe as possible should war ever reach Singapore. He wanted them all to eventually be able to return to the lives they had known in New Zealand.

The next morning John was on the flight line early, pre-flighting the Buffalo he was soon to take up to get some air experience in the aircraft. After forty minutes of poking around the machine, he was satisfied it was ready for flight. Looking at it, he saw how squat and rounded the aeroplane was. No aerodynamic beauty, he decided, wistfully thinking of his Spitfire. He had read the Buffalo handling notes and gone through the aircraft's flight manual the previous night, so he was satisfied he was as well prepared as he could be for his first flight in the aircraft.

As he sat in the high cockpit, John noted the large radial engine was not the impediment the longer engine cowlings of the Spitfire had been to a pilot's forward visibility on the ground. Certainly, care would be needed when taxiing, but he would be able to see ground obstructions reasonably well from the Buffalo. As he looked around the inside of the cockpit, John noted there were four small windows low down, nearly level with his knees. They were there to provide a pilot with some view directly below the aircraft, the only direction not easily viewable from a cockpit that otherwise provided good visibility all around. After spending a few minutes getting himself comfortable with the position of the various switches and levers in the cockpit, John set about starting the engine. He had read the engine needed four or five strokes on the primer pump when it was cold.

'All right, starting procedure, John,' he said to himself. 'Ignition to both; build fuel pressure; push in the starter switch; hold it in for fifteen seconds... Thousand and one, thousand and two, thousand and three...' he counted, using his preferred method for estimating one second. At one thousand and fifteen, he pulled the switch out. The engine caught and fired up. John released the switch and it returned to its neutral position.

After the engine had warmed up, John checked his switches, temperatures, and pressures, and ensured his control surfaces responded correctly to inputs on the control stick. Then he ran up the engine to test it under power and exercise the propellor pitch mechanism. Being held on its brakes at high power caused the aircraft to jerk and buck. *Pressure and temps in the green. I'm ready to go,* John thought.

There was no radio call to make as he prepared to take off. The Buffalos had no radios fitted. Apparently, this was to be rectified within the next week, but the absence of radios was another sign of the poor state of Singapore's air defence capability, John decided. He checked for other traffic. 'Nothing in the air, downwind, base, or final,' John recited to himself. Neither were there any other aircraft on the ground. He taxied on to the strip and pushed in the throttle to accelerate the Buffalo for take-off. The aircraft began to swing to the left, reacting to the engine's torque and propellor slipstream. John stopped the swing by firmly pressing the aircraft's right rudder pedal. The control stick felt lethargic and heavy. This was not a sprightly aeroplane. He had to push the stick forward with some force to help lift the aircraft's tail as his speed increased. *God, if I had been that brutal in my Spitfire, I would have put my prop into the ground*, he thought.

As soon as he was airborne, with a positive rate of climb, John raised the undercarriage and reduced engine boost from its take-off setting. He set his propellor to 2,400 revolutions and continued climbing at an indicated airspeed of 145mph. He planned to climb to six thousand feet and run through a series of air exercises.

Level at six thousand feet in a cloudless sky, and some fifteen miles out over a deep blue South China Sea, John set about his air exercises. Some gentle turns left and right, followed by some steep turns in both directions, told him that while the controls were not very light, nor precise, the aircraft could be flown accurately. It just required firm inputs.

He decided to try stalls next. He reduced power and held the nose up at an ever-increasing angle as his speed washed off. At seventy-five miles per hour, the aircraft shuddered momentarily and then dropped its nose steeply as it entered an aerodynamic stall. John recovered in the usual way, by checking the control stick forward, powering up, and recovering in the climb.

Time for a fully developed stall, he decided. *Need to ensure no spin occurs. This aircraft isn't approved for spinning.* He reduced engine boost, but continued to carry some power into this stalling exercise. He lowered the flaps to one third down, as shown on the visual indicator at the bottom of the main instrument panel. The control column felt imprecise. *Soggy*, he thought, *even allowing for my low airspeed.*

The aircraft's speed continued to reduce as John held the Buffalo's nose above the line of the distant horizon. Then it happened. At an indicated airspeed of seventy miles per hour, there was a shudder through the airframe, followed by a loud bang. The left wing dropped sharply as the aircraft's nose fell steeply below the horizon, slicing down towards the left as it went. John was about to enter a spin. He checked the control stick forward, stood on the right rudder pedal to stop the nose continuing left, and added power. It was an ungainly recovery by the Buffalo, but it slowly responded to John's control movements, and the incipient spin it had entered came to nothing. It was an unpleasant experience; John was used to much finer responses and more effective controls after his Spitfire time. *Young Giles was right; this machine is a dog*, John thought.

After landing back at Kallang, John shut the aircraft down and climbed out. Looking back at it as he walked to the air operations room, he decided it flew in a way he would have expected from such a heavy, blunt-looking aeroplane. That is, not well at all.

Later that day, John sat down with Richard Stark to discuss and plan a training schedule for the squadron pilots.

'Flight Lieutenant, having now flown the Buffalo, I can see we are going to be tested if we have the misfortune to end up flying against the Zeros of the Imperial Japanese Army Air Force. I had heard the Buffalo's performance was sub-standard, and having flown it this morning, I can confirm that's an accurate assessment. Worryingly, I wasn't even trying the extreme manoeuvres we expect in combat. I think it could move from being a sub-standard aircraft to just bloody dangerous in active war service.'

Richard stayed silent but nodded in agreement.

'We need to get the promised Hurricanes here as soon as we can,' John continued. 'Who at HQ Singapore can help me message Britain about the urgent need for capable aircraft if the squadron is to have effective air capability? We just won't be able to do it with Buffalos.'

'General Simpson is the person you need to see, sir. He's in charge of equipment logistics for all three services here.'

'Right. Organise a time for me to see him. Soonest opportunity, please. Tell his people it's an urgent matter. Also, I want to reconnoitre the local area from the air today, to understand the geography and general lie of the land. I will take two pilots with me to form a flight of three. I thought Flying Officers Roberts and Salt. Could you have them report here in an hour, to join me on the recce? Thank you, Flight Lieutenant.'

Just under two hours later, three Buffalos from 48 Squadron took off from RAF Kallang. Once clear of the aerodrome area, they formed into an echelon right formation running off John's starboard wing, operating with the fifty-yard lateral spacing between aircraft John had briefed the other two pilots about, before take-off.

'This is a general recce, principally to help me orientate myself and understand the geography of the area,' John had told them during the pre-flight briefing. 'Airborne, we will climb to five thousand as we track towards Tekong Island and on across the Malay peninsula. I want to run up the east coast for about a hundred miles, to Endau, then west across the peninsula to Malacca, and back down the other side to Kallang.'

'Are we looking for anything in particular, sir?' Don had asked.

'No, it's just a familiarisation flight, so I can actually see positions noted on our maps and check the topography.'

Now, crossing Tekong Island, John could see the beginnings of the rainforest on the Malay Peninsula, just a short distance ahead. It became very dense, very quickly. He recalled what he'd been told by a senior army officer he had spoken to during his brief stay in Cairo, who had been describing why Singapore was seen as such a stronghold for Britain. The officer had explained that the sea approaches from the east, west and south were all protected by the British navy and some big guns installed on shore. He assured John that nothing was going to come down from the north that would cause concern, since that was impenetrable jungle.

As John looked down, he could see that the jungle was dense, but he was not entirely convinced that it was impenetrable.

Thirty-five minutes later, the three Buffalos turned west as they flew over the town of Endau, which John saw was situated at the mouth of a large river. They were now headed for Malacca. *No place for an engine failure*, John thought as he looked at the terrain they were flying over. The trees down there looked tall and solid. He found himself checking his gauges to ensure all was well up front, under the cowls.

The remainder of the flight was uneventful, and the three aircraft were soon lining up for their landing approach back at Kallang. John landed first, and as he turned to taxi to the ready area, he saw Don's aircraft touching down. Trevor was approaching behind him. He looked low, given his distance from the strip threshold. *Give it some power, Trevor,* John thought, but Trevor continued to sink below what John considered to be the correct approach profile. There were some low, but substantial, trees off the threshold, and Trevor was sinking at such a rate that he was in danger of colliding with them. But without a radio, John could not warn him. He felt helpless as he watched Trevor's aircraft continue to sink below the required path.

Then he saw that power had been applied. The Buffalo began to climb, but very slowly. Trevor had clearly realised that he had misjudged his approach, and he was going around to make a second approach and landing. But John could see he was not climbing fast enough. His undercarriage was still down and his flaps remained at landing setting, creating a lot of unnecessary drag. It was preventing him from establishing an adequate climb.

'Get your gear and flaps up, man!' John called out in frustration. As if in response, Trevor's undercarriage began to retract and his flaps began moving back up to the wing's trailing edge. Climbing under full power, Trevor passed over the treetops with no more than fifty feet to spare. If there had been any further delay, the Buffalo would have hit the trees.

'Christ almighty,' John muttered to himself. 'We have some work to do.'

CHAPTER FIVE

The following day, John ushered his second-in-command, Richard, into a quiet corner of the mess hall. 'We need to get the pilots underway with more air exercises as soon as we can,' he told him. 'When my flight was landing after our recce flight yesterday, Flying Officer Roberts was much too low and slow on approach. He nearly hit the trees about one hundred yards short of the landing threshold.'

'Yes, I heard about that, sir. It wasn't good. Those trees can be a hazard when landing on that vector.'

'The trees are quite avoidable and not a major problem if approaches are flown properly. My worry, Flight Lieutenant, is that Flying Officer Roberts allowed his aircraft to get into an unsafe situation, and he almost crashed as a result. He made no corrective action until it was almost too late, and then he just scraped out of it. Why didn't he recognise his problem earlier and do something about it, before it became so critical?'

'I've spoken to him, sir. The situation took him by surprise,' Richard responded. 'The conditions were not difficult, but he overlooked a couple of things. The winds were light, but temperature and humidity were high, ninety-six degrees and ninety per cent respectively. He overlooked the effect that would have on his lift, didn't carry sufficient power nor maintain his speed, and consequently the aircraft's sink-rate got away from him.'

'You may be correct, but a properly trained pilot based here in the tropics should not be making such a mistake. I think the problem is that we have inexperienced people flying the Buffalo, which is not a pilot-friendly aircraft at any time. It's easy to make a mistake in it, and if you do, it is unforgiving. I want the chaps up flying their aircraft every day. They are to practise take-offs and landings, including crosswind exercises, formation flying, and basic combat manoeuvres. The manoeuvres should be at a higher level initially, and then tried at low level as the pilots get more comfortable. The density altitude issues we suffer in this climate will play a role as they push their aircraft to the edge of the operating envelope, so the men need to be aware of that, and factor it into their decision-making. I want every pilot to get to the point where they are unlikely to be surprised by what the aircraft may do, or not do, in all flight regimes, at all heights.'

'I will develop a comprehensive training timetable for your approval, sir,' Richard replied.

'Thank you, Flight Lieutenant. Not only do I want the pilots of this squadron flying well enough to avoid the sort of poor performance I saw in this case, but I also want them in top form in case the worst happens and we find ourselves at war with the Japanese.'

'It will be good to get our Hurricanes here sooner rather than later if we are going to be at war with Japan.'

'They have been promised, but no-one can tell me when they will arrive, or confirm how many there will be,' John told him. 'I'm chasing the issue and have put a request in to meet General Simpson, who oversees equipment provision, including aircraft. I want him to send through a "Most Urgent" request to Fighter Command in Britain. I'm not having any luck getting an appointment with him at this stage, let alone trying to persuade him to push for the promised Hurricanes.'

'I might be able to help, sir. I know a young lady who works in his office. She's secretarial but gets on with the General well and might be able to arrange a quick meeting for you.'

'I'll try anything. See what she can do, would you? A simple brief for her when she talks to her boss: the CO of Forty-Eight Squadron is very keen to meet him regarding the provision of Hurricanes due to be sent out to Singapore from Britain.'

Early the next day, John and Richard met in John's office to discuss the training plan Richard had drafted overnight. It was exactly what John wanted. The squadron would undertake a range of special exercises, operating on each occasion as three separate flights, designated A, B, and C. The flights would comprise four aircraft each. Every day, each flight would take on one task, involving a particular exercise chosen from the menu of training activities Richard had put together.

On day one, A Flight was to be on circuits and landings, B Flight was to practise formation flying in both level flight and when climbing or descending, and C Flight would undertake some upper air exercises — stalling, steep turning, and some basic combat manoeuvring. Days two and three would see the flights move through the other exercises in turn, so that every three days the squadron would complete one whole training exercise rotation. John was pleased. He thought that after two or three cycles through each of the exercises, the pilots' skills in the Buffalo should have improved substantially. Then they could move on to the serious stuff he had planned — advanced air combat manoeuvres.

'That's fine, thank you, Flight Lieutenant,' he approved. 'I will lead A Flight. You take B, and I presume Flying Officer Salt should take C, being the other qualified instructor?'

'Yes, sir, that's correct.'

'Okay, that's it then. Could you and Flying Officer Salt meet me here at fourteen hundred hours? We will refine the exercise content, allocate pilots to flights, and get the programme ready to roll.'

'Very well, sir, shall do. Oh, by the way, my friend in the General's office says that if you can go by his rooms at eleven-fifty tomorrow, he can give you five minutes. That's all, apparently. He's due at Raffles for a senior officers' lunch at twelve-thirty.'

Ah, the lifestyle of the commanders in this colonial outpost, John thought. *Very comfortable. Let's hope there is enough of a sense of urgency for those in charge to make some decisions about what must be done to ensure we are best placed to cope with anything Japan may try.*

'Good morning, Squadron Leader Noble,' said General Simpson when John presented himself at the appointed time. 'One of my staff says you are anxious to see me on some matter regarding air capability. I can give you a few minutes only. I'm due at a function soon.'

'Good morning, General Simpson. Thank you for making time.' John said nothing about the fact his earlier formal requests for a meeting had got him nowhere.

'So, what is it you wish to raise with me?'

'I'm the Commanding Officer of Forty-Eight Squadron, RNZAF. I am RAF, but I've been seconded down here to help develop local fighter aircraft capability.'

'Is there an issue with our capability? We have plenty of aircraft on Singapore Island.'

'We do, sir, but the aircraft are of a type that may be inadequate in battle, so effectiveness in the air is uncertain. If the Japanese launch any air attack against Singapore, we can deal with the bombers, but they will have fighter protection, mostly Zeros, and they will be able to out-gun and out-fly our Buffalo aircraft.'

'It's a pretty serious suggestion to make, Squadron Leader, that our air force here on the island is inadequate against Japanese fighters, if it ever comes to that.'

'I appreciate what you say, sir, but that's my judgement. As well as having an aircraft type that I believe will struggle against Japanese fighters, I have pilots who are not experienced flyers, let alone in air warfare. We are busy with training programmes that will help their personal proficiency improve, but they will struggle against the Japanese because they will be in an inferior aircraft.'

'I don't like to hear a British officer admitting to likely defeat before anything even starts, Squadron Leader. Not good for morale, in my view, and not something that should be said.'

John could feel his anger growing, but he knew better than to show it. Confrontation was not the way to progress his issue. 'I understand that, sir, and I would never be public about my view on aircraft capability. That would be counterproductive. I'm busy trying to bring flying skills up to a better level, but our chances of being successful in air defence operations are poor. Our chances would be enhanced if the Hurricanes I was promised as I was leaving Britain could be obtained as soon as possible.'

'What's your experience to allow you to say all this, Squadron Leader?'

'My judgement on flight personnel and aircraft capability is based on my last two years as an operational Spitfire pilot in Britain. I flew at Dunkirk and through the Battle of Britain.'

'Ah, now I see. Come to show us how it's done, have you? One of Churchill's *Few*, so you know what's what. Well, let me tell you, Squadron Leader, we think we are well set up to defend ourselves in the unlikely event the Japanese come this way. We have more than seventy fighter aircraft on the island

and more on the mainland. There are capital ships being sent here, and we have nearly ninety thousand troops in Malaya. Our present aircraft will enable your chaps, if you train them well, to offer the air defence we need if the Japanese arrive.'

'Sir —' John began, but he was interrupted.

'I haven't finished, Squadron Leader. If Hurricanes were promised, then they will turn up at some point. I don't see the need to panic and fire off any urgent requests. You also shouldn't forget the United States has a very large presence in the Pacific. The Japanese aren't going to be able to try anything down in this part of the world without coming up against the US, so I think it's unlikely you and your pilots will have to face Japanese aircraft any time soon, if ever.'

'All I ask, sir, is that you reaffirm the request for the Hurricanes and seek early delivery, given the risks Singapore may face.'

'No, I won't do that, Squadron Leader. I don't share your sense of urgency, nor do I accept we are as poorly placed for air operations as you suggest. Now, I must go. Luncheon calls.'

John was furious but said nothing. He recognised that the General's response was driven by complacency and his comfortable belief in British superiority in Asia. *Some of the senior officers here live in another world,* he thought, *too busy enjoying their colonial lifestyle. They probably wouldn't know how to respond to any sudden war emergency, anyway.*

Some ten days after his unproductive meeting with General Simpson, John was in his office with Richard, discussing the squadron's training progress. The pilots had all now completed three cycles of each of the exercise types in the plan.

'It's going well, sir, as you will have seen with your own flight. The incident rate has been zero, and there is no doubt in my mind we are seeing a different quality of flying.'

'Yes,' John agreed, 'I've seen it. Good anticipation, good decision-making, and good execution in the air. There's no doubt they have progressed.'

'I suggest a day off tomorrow. Don't want them feeling worn down because it's so constant. Let them have a day to refresh and come back keen?'

'Good suggestion, Flight Lieutenant. Advise them tomorrow is theirs, to relax and do whatever. In your memo to them about it, make a comment about the good progress they are making, and say I am pleased with the way it's going. Nothing like a bit of recognition and encouragement. We will move to more advanced aerial warfare training when we recommence.'

'Very well, sir. Also, the radio equipment to go into each aircraft has finally arrived after being unexpectedly delayed. It's being installed as we speak and should be finished late tomorrow, so a day off suits from that perspective as well.'

'I'm very pleased to hear that. I couldn't believe our aircraft had no radios installed when I first arrived.'

'I shall let the pilots know your view on training progress, as you ask, and I will also let them know that their advanced air combat training is next. They will like that. Another thing, sir: Flying Officer Salt and I might have a hit at the golf course tomorrow. Just nine holes — too hot for much more. Would you be interested in joining us? The course isn't far away. It's up by the reservoir. We just hire clubs.'

'I didn't know there was a golf course that handy, but yes — I'm a starter, thanks.'

'Good-oh. Thought we would tee off early, before the heat builds. The car will pick us up at o-eight-hundred.'

'That's fine. Thank you.'

John thought a day off would be good for the pilots, and a round on the golf course for him would be an enjoyable break. He had played some golf before, on a casual basis back home in New Zealand. He did not play enough to have a handicap, but his game was passable.

John, Richard, and Don had finished eight of their planned nine holes when they caught up with the group of four playing ahead of them. The four were very slow and seemed to be arguing about the application of local rules. Clearly not a casual round, John decided. As he watched them, he recognised one of the players as General Simpson.

The general's group moved off down the fairway after they had teed off from hole nine. The general himself appeared to have sliced his drive into some trees, and he was poking around looking for his ball on the right-hand side of the fairway. His fellow players were further along the course, walking towards their balls, which had gone to the left-hand side.

'There's General Simpson,' John said, 'the target of my unsuccessful attempt to remind Command back in Britain that we need our new Hurricanes sooner rather than later. He wasn't interested in even sending a signal enquiring about delivery. He implied my criticism of current aircraft and systems was disloyal.'

'Should have warned you, sir, sorry. He has a reputation for being stubborn and narrowly focused. He's hard to move on most things, let alone something big like aircraft upgrades. He loves Singapore and its lifestyle. I think he's got special membership at Raffles, his second home,' Richard said.

'Look at what he's doing!' Don exclaimed. The three pilots all craned forward, trying to follow what was happening.

The general had found his ball, but instead of playing it from where it lay in the trees and undergrowth, he had kicked it clear, onto the fairway. Now, he was preparing to play his next shot from there, as if that was where it had originally landed.

'What a damn cheat,' Don said.

'Unbelievable. Very poor form,' Richard agreed.

The golf clubroom was largely empty when John and his playing partners came in. A couple of groups were having lunch before teeing off, but that was it, apart from General Simpson and his friends, who were all having a drink at the bar after finishing their round.

As John walked past, he acknowledged the general with a quiet, 'Hello, sir.'

Clearly uncertain who John was, General Simpson looked at him blankly for a moment before recognition dawned. 'Oh, hello, Squadron Leader,' he said. 'I didn't know you were a golfer. Anyway, what are you doing here? I thought you were busy training your pilots to improve their performance in your Buffalos.'

'We are well underway with that, sir. It's our day off today.'

'Very good. I've just had a win with my friends here. We always have a small wager. I cleaned them up this morning, so that will pay for my gins for the rest of the week.'

'Congratulations sir.' Then John had a thought. 'Could I have a private word?'

'Not now, Squadron Leader. Inappropriate time to talk about military issues,' the general responded, winking at his friends.

'It would be in both our best interests if you could give me a moment, sir.'

'All right. One minute, and it better be important. You're interfering with my golf day,' he said as he stepped away with John. 'Well, Squadron Leader?'

'I was very disappointed you wouldn't take the time to send a signal about the replacement aircraft we need as a matter of urgency.'

'Yes, I understand that, but you have my answer. Now, is there anything else? I wish to rejoin my companions and continue our match analysis. That will help them understand why I won their money today,' he said with a chuckle.

'Yes, sir, there is. One of the wonderful things about the game of golf is the sense of fellowship it creates between those playing together. I think the trust and confidence that exists between fellow players contributes to that. You know your playing partners will do the right thing, like being quiet while someone plays their shot, or keeping an accurate count of the strokes they play.'

'Why are you giving me this exposition, Squadron Leader?'

'I was thinking, sir, of how poorly someone would be thought of if they cheated by doing something extraordinarily out of order while engaged in a round. Imagine, for example, if one of the members of your group had landed their ball in the trees when teeing off from hole nine. Then, instead of playing the ball from a difficult lie, or treating it as unplayable and taking a penalty, they surreptitiously kicked it back onto the fairway and played from that better position, as if nothing had happened? That could happen if a player was dishonest and thought he could get away with it because his playing partners were not in a position from where they could observe what he was doing. Of course, anyone doing that would have to be confident no-one had seen him, including, say, the players coming up behind.'

The general went pale. He swallowed nervously but said nothing.

'As bad as such dreadful behaviour would be, it would not really be any of my business if I had observed it,' John went on. 'I have more pressing matters in mind, such as chasing Command in Britain over the promised Hurricanes. That's my real concern. Much more important than getting sidetracked by who did what in a casual golf match between friends. Do you see how I'm thinking, sir?'

For a moment the general remained silent. Then he said, rather stiffly, 'I understand your perspective completely, Squadron Leader. Just so you know, I will be sending an urgent request to Command tomorrow, enquiring about delivery dates for replacements for the Buffalos, and emphasising our need to upgrade aircraft. Now, I must rejoin my playing partners.'

'Thank you, sir. Much appreciated,' John replied with a nod. Then he made his way back to where Richard and Don were drinking their beers.

'Long chat with the general,' Richard said.

'Yes, I was just following up on him pressing for the Hurricanes. He's going to send a signal tomorrow.'

'Oh, that's very good news. How on earth did you move him to that? I thought he had turned you down.'

'I talked to him about the sanctity of trust and integrity in golf. For example, how bad it would be if someone cheated by kicking a ball out of a difficult position for their next shot. I indicated it wasn't something that needed to be talked about when there were more important things affecting us at present. He agreed and told me he would take up the issue of replacement aircraft when back in his office.'

'Well done, sir,' Richard responded, a huge grin on his face.

CHAPTER SIX

Over the following weeks, the training of 48 Squadron pilots continued apace. John was satisfied that good progress was being made in air warfare training. The pilots were showing good intuition in their dogfighting manoeuvres, and they were handling the Buffalos well in all flight regimes. Previously, some of the men had looked apprehensive as they made their way to the waiting aircraft, but now their new confidence was showing on their faces.

'They all seem to have lifted their level of competence in recent weeks,' John said to Richard and Don. They were meeting in John's office to review training progress. 'I'm certainly happy with everyone in A Flight. Are you both confident about those in your flights?'

'Yes. B Flight's fine. I have no concerns about anyone,' Richard responded.

'Same for C Flight, sir,' Don said, 'although I have noted that Pilot Officer Kemp can become a bit flustered when required to do something quickly. We had a mock scramble last week, and I could see the pressure of doing everything at speed was causing him a few issues. Nothing serious, but nevertheless it signalled that he has some work to do. He's not entirely comfortable.'

'What did he do?' John asked.

'Well, he was in such a hurry he got his starting sequence wrong and consequently had trouble getting his engine to fire. The result was him sitting there by himself, struggling to start, while the rest of the flight was taking off in response to the scramble order. That made it worse for him, I think, because when he did finally get his engine started, he proceeded to take off with the wrong flap setting, and his aircraft wouldn't climb properly as a consequence. I think he was too keen to get moving and catch up with the others, and that caused him to make mistakes. I've seen it before from young Kemp. He gets a bit flummoxed when he's under pressure.'

'What's your recommendation?'

'He just needs a bit more exposure to the Buffalo, sir. I plan to give him some extra attention on training exercises. I'm reasonably confident he will come right with more time in the aircraft. He's one of our less experienced pilots, so we shouldn't be too hard on him. We know what a cow of an aircraft the Buffalo is, even for a capable pilot.'

'Very well. I would like to have a look at how he flies, so swap him into my Flight tomorrow, would you?'

'Will do.'

'Now, the plan from here is to intensify the whole of squadron ops, including formation climbs to altitude and dogfighting exercises. It's the type of flying we will be required to undertake in any war situation: climbing to meet the enemy and engaging on interception. We'll do it with everyone involved, rather than dividing into the separate flights we've been using for exercises to date.'

'Do we have any update from HQ regarding the Japanese threat, sir?' Richard asked. 'I've read in the paper there are concerns about what the Japanese are saying regarding the oil embargo. Apparently, there's been some suggestion by one politician in Tokyo that they may have to take the initiative, to bring the issue to an end. God knows what that means, but it's a worry that they're talking like that.'

'Nothing definite, but you're right. Some of the statements coming out of Tokyo are seen by Malayan Command as concerning,' John replied, 'particularly now that Tojo is in charge after pushing the former Japanese PM out. He's demanding the US stop providing aid to China and lift the oil embargo against Japan. He says if that's agreed, Japan will promise not to launch any attacks in Southeast Asia and will pull out of Indochina.'

'Why are the Japanese even talking about the possibility of launching attacks in this region? It shows it's under consideration, don't you think?' Richard asked.

'The view at the top is that if the US turns Tojo down, the risk of wider Japanese aggression does increase substantially. I understand British forces are about to be moved to a state of readiness throughout Malaya, just in case.'

'Well, if the United States is driving the negotiations with Japan, we have some comfort from their presence in the Pacific. They have a bloody big navy, with some of it based at Pearl Harbor in Hawaii. That should be on the minds of the Japanese.'

'Correct,' John responded, 'and as you know, the Royal Navy is sending a couple of capital ships out here as well, to show a stronger British presence: the *Prince of Wales* and the *Repulse*.'

'Surely the Japanese wouldn't want to take on Britain and the States?' Don queried.

'Let's hope not. In the meantime, we train and prepare, just in case. I would be happier if our Hurricanes were here. Meeting the Japanese in our Buffalos, if that's where this gets to, is far from optimum,' John said with a grimace.

The twelve Buffalos from 48 Squadron climbed in formation as they headed south, out over the sea from RAF Kallang. John had specified a formation climb to seventeen thousand feet in three flights of four aircraft each. Each flight was flying as a *schwarm*, a technique used by the Luftwaffe and adopted by some British squadrons during the Battle of Britain. It involved four aircraft flying together as a group, effectively in two pairs. Each pair, when engaging in aerial combat, would operate as a separate unit, comprising the leader and his wingman. John had found pairs to be a very effective formation for dogfighting against the Luftwaffe, and had now established it as the default technique for his squadron in Singapore.

As they climbed, John once again found himself contemplating the inadequacies of the Buffalo. It did not perform well at altitude, its engine tended to overheat, and there had been more reports of fuel starvation at height. Coupled with its poor handling and general unreliability, the aircraft made life extremely difficult for a squadron commander trying to prepare to meet an opponent with superior aircraft and, probably, more experienced pilots. As the squadron was climbing through fifteen thousand feet, John's thoughts were interrupted. There was a call from one of the pilots in B Flight, which was operating as Yellow Section for today's exercise. John could hear the urgency in his voice.

'Yellow One, this is Yellow Three. I'm overheating. Gauges are in the red. Reducing power.'

John glanced behind him, to his right, where B Flight was positioned. The leader of the second pair in that flight was dropping down, out of the formation, obviously unable to maintain either speed or rate of climb.

Richard, leading B Flight as Yellow One, responded immediately. 'Yellow Three, break away and return to base.'

Good, thought John. *That's the right call. The damn engine might fail at any time or even catch fire. Don't want to end up in that.* He looked down at the large expanse of water below. Like all the others, he had heard the stories of the shark-infested South China Sea. No-one wanted to be forced down there.

A few minutes later, the squadron levelled at seventeen thousand feet. John was about to call the beginning of the briefed exercise, when there was another call. This time, it was one of his flight.

'Red One, Red Two is misfiring. It's intermittent. I think it's fuel starvation.'

'Have you tried the auxiliary pump?'

'Affirmative. No change. Returning to Kallang.'

'Roger, Red Two. See you later.'

Red Two, flown by Pilot Officer Kemp immediately on John's right as his wingman, rolled into a sweeping, descending turn, heading back to their aerodrome on the now distant Singapore Island.

Forty-five minutes later, John called a halt to the dogfighting exercises they were practising, making the standard call used by the squadron to signal termination of air exercises. 'Red One to squadron: knock it off. Proceeding back to base.' With that, John turned his aircraft towards Singapore and began slowly descending towards RAF Kallang. The remainder of the squadron followed.

'Where's Pilot Officer Kemp?' John asked when he was back at the base. He had landed fifteen minutes ago and had seen no sign of the pilot officer's aircraft. The other Buffalo that had returned early was there, but not his. *Must be in the maintenance hangar*, John decided.

He walked to the hangar, planning to talk to the chief flight engineer about what may be causing fuel starvation issues. He suspected vaporisation due to the hot conditions, but he needed clarification. John was also keen to talk to Pilot Officer

Kemp, but his Buffalo was not in the maintenance hangar when he got there. He asked the flight engineer if he had seen it.

'I don't know where Pilot Officer Kemp's aircraft is, sir. He hasn't been in here today,' the flight engineer replied.

John felt a growing sense of unease. The Buffalo flown by Kemp was not anywhere on Kallang aerodrome, he now knew. He arranged for the duty sergeant in the ops room to check with the other RAF aerodromes, at Tengah and Seletar. Perhaps he had diverted to one of those airfields, although John doubted it, as they were further from where they had been flying than Kallang.

'Pilot Officer Kemp is missing,' John said to Richard, who was in the main flight administration office as John came in. 'He wasn't here when we landed. I've had the other aerodromes checked, but he's not at either of them. We need to get some aircraft up to search along his assumed track back to Kallang. Also, get ops to contact control to see if there's been any report of an aircraft down somewhere on the island. In the meantime, you, me, and Flying Officer Salt will make an aerial search along the track he would have followed. Get Flying Officer Salt here, please, and I'll brief our mission before launching.'

When Don had arrived, John launched into his brief.

'We were south of Sugi Island when Red Two broke away to return. He had about seventy miles to run from there to Kallang. If he's gone down in the sea, we'll be lucky to find him.'

'And if he did go down on one of the small islands along his assumed route, because it's mostly dense tropical forest, any aircraft crashing through the tree canopy there would just disappear,' Don said.

'This was our estimated position when he left us to return to base,' John went on as he marked a point on the map spread out on the table in front of them. 'I've drawn a line from there to the aerodrome, showing his assumed track home. He should be somewhere along the line.'

Richard and Don agreed.

'Okay, if you're ready we'll get airborne and start looking for him. We will operate with call-signs Search One, Two, and Three. I'm One, Flight Lieutenant Stark can be Two, and Flying Officer Salt, you are Three. Outbound from Kallang, I plan to fly the reciprocal of the track we think Pilot Officer Kemp followed as he came back, right out to the position we were at when he experienced the issue that caused him to turn around. Search height is to be two thousand feet. That keeps us low enough to see any sign of his aircraft, but high enough to allow a relatively wide scan. Over any terrain, we will increase our height as necessary to maintain two thousand feet above the surface.'

'Are we going to expand the search laterally?' Richard asked.

'Yes, no point in us being closed-up as we fly along the track we are searching. I want you a mile east of me, Flight Lieutenant, and you, Flying Officer Salt, please fly a mile out on the western side. Flying a precise line is never easy over the sea, without reference points, but I will stick to the compass heading that will keep me close to the track we want to follow. That should work — there's not much wind. You both just parallel my flight path. That's our task outbound. If we reach the position at which Pilot Officer Kemp left us, and we've had no sighting of interest, we will fly our return search leg slightly differently.'

Richard and Don looked at him expectantly.

'We will follow return tracks that provide wider coverage. I want a six-mile search swathe as we come back, rather than the two miles we'll use for our outbound sweep. That will mean more area is covered, but it will affect our ability to scan in the same detail. So, it's a close pattern search as we go out, looking for any sign of Pilot Officer Kemp or his aeroplane, and a wider pattern as we come back in. The Catalina Search and Rescue crews use the same protocol, and they say it's the best compromise on SAR missions. I want to keep speed lower than normal cruise while we search. We will use one-eighty miles per hour. Don't want to be any faster than that. A higher speed would make it harder to spot something.'

'Got it,' Richard acknowledged.

'Okay, let's go,' John said, leading the way outside to the three waiting Buffalos the ground crew had refuelled and prepared for the search mission.

After take-off into the northerly breeze, John led the Buffalos into a gentle climbing turn to the left, passing the city's all-important reservoirs slightly to their west, and flying over the Tanglin Barracks and, just after that, the area John knew housed the British Forces HQ. He levelled at two thousand feet as they crossed the coastline and moved out into the Singapore Strait.

'Search One is on the search track. Two and Three, take up your respective positions now.'

As John watched, Richard rolled his aircraft to the left and positioned himself about a mile out from John, paralleling his line of flight to the east. Don banked right, establishing himself a mile west of John. Soon they were crossing a large unnamed island, lying to the west of Batam Island. They increased their altitude to preserve a two-thousand-foot margin over its terrain. Each of them peered down at the tree-covered areas below, looking for unusual gaps in the forest canopy or any other sign of disruption.

Twenty minutes later, the flight of searching Buffalos was well out over the South China Sea, with the higher peaks of Sumatra now showing clearly to their west. There had been no sign of the missing Buffalo. John was becoming increasingly concerned. He knew that if Pilot Officer Kemp had come down in the sea, his aircraft would not stay afloat for long. Survival in the open ocean, even if the pilot was wearing flotation equipment, was never guaranteed after two hours.

Suddenly, Richard called on his radio. 'Search One, this is Two. I see something in the water. My two o'clock, about a third of the way towards your search line track.'

John scanned the area described by Richard but could not see anything. 'Negative contact. Go in and have a closer look, Search Two. I will orbit in my current position. Search Three, you orbit in your position.'

John saw Richard turn slightly right and begin descending. Then he lost sight of him as he continued in his own orbit. Impatient to be able to see what was happening, John steepened the angle of his bank to come around more quickly. He soon saw Richard at about four hundred feet above the sea surface, circling a small area of the ocean. Even though he now knew exactly where to look, he still could not see what it was Richard had spotted.

'Got something in the water there, Search Two?' John called on the radio.

'Yes, I think we've found him,' Richard responded, but he did not sound excited. 'I will vacate the area to the east. You come in and have a look, and let me know if you see what I think I've seen.'

John reduced his power, slowed to one hundred and twenty miles per hour, lowered his flaps slightly, and descended gently towards the area where Richard had been circling something he had seen in the water. John saw it as he got closer. Floating on the surface were small pieces of what looked like the remains of an aircraft's tail. *It's the right shape for it to be from a Buffalo*, John decided, as he took in other bits of flotsam on the water that were now more obvious.

As he peered down, John's attention was drawn to something light-yellow in colour, bobbing near the floating pieces of wreckage. Dropping his left wing down to open his view as he passed overhead, he confirmed that it was a Mae West life-jacket. He could also see the head and shoulders of the person wearing it, face-down in the water. He peered closely and gagged. There was nothing from the waist down. The lower half of the body was gone. He saw two black shadows circling the remains. Sharks. As he watched, there was a flurry of white water around the Mae West. One of the sharks turned quickly in towards Pilot Officer Kemp's body, and its huge mouth opened, its head jerking back and forth as it seized and ripped away more flesh.

'That is Buffalo wreckage in the water, and a body. We've found him, and he hasn't survived,' John called, trying not to let any emotion into his voice. It was difficult, finding a fellow pilot dead, especially in the circumstances he had just seen, but he was in command. He knew he had to be professional and stay on top of his emotions. 'Search Two and Three, form up on me. Returning to base, climbing six thousand.'

The pilots did not speak as they flew back to Kallang.

Back on the ground, John asked Richard and Don to accompany him to the administration office. A young woman was laboriously typing some maintenance records as the three pilots entered.

'I need the room. Would you mind getting yourself a cool drink for ten minutes?'

The WAAF left hurriedly, obviously recognising trouble when she saw it.

John turned to Richard and Don. 'Gentlemen, as you know, we've lost Pilot Officer Kemp. We saw wreckage that clearly came from his Buffalo, and we saw his body in the water. Flying Officer Salt, you didn't see what Flight Lieutenant Stark and I saw, but I regret to have to say that Pilot Officer Kemp had been savaged by sharks. There was nothing left of him from the waist down.'

'Oh, Christ,' Don reacted, turning pale.

'I don't want the details of what has happened to Pilot Officer Kemp to become the subject of undue discussion among the pilots. We have a difficult enough time ahead of us as it is, if the Japanese launch any attack. I want to avoid having the pilots worry about being attacked by sharks if they end up in the sea. So, we will be advising the squadron members only that Pilot Officer Kemp crashed into the South China Sea as he returned early from an exercise when his aircraft malfunctioned, that our search and rescue exercise found the wreckage of his aircraft, and that his body was observed floating face-down nearby, clearly deceased.'

'Fair enough. Hopefully he was already dead before the sharks attacked him,' Richard replied.

'Of course, absolutely,' Don added in a wavering voice.

'Thank you, gentlemen. I will be reporting the aircraft and pilot lost, the circumstances of his turn-back, the fact that wreckage and his body have been spotted well out at sea, and that no recovery is proposed.'

No useful purpose would be served in trying to recover Pilot Officer Kemp's remains, even if they could locate them again, and John was conscious of the fact that Malayan Command had indicated, as part of its war-planning, that it was impractical to try to recover bodies of airmen shot down at sea. Recovery missions would not be authorised. If a downed pilot was found alive, a flying boat may be able to land near them and retrieve, but that was the only situation in which such a mission would be undertaken.

CHAPTER SEVEN

By the end of November, it was clear to everyone in Singapore that war was inevitable in Southeast Asia. It was just a question of when and where the Japanese would strike.

John was satisfied with the progress of the squadron pilots. Their intensive training programme was paying off, but he still worried about the equipment available. Outdated Brewster Buffalos, no matter how well flown, would struggle against the more advanced Japanese fighter aircraft. John continued to hound RAF HQ in Singapore, pressing for the Hurricanes he had been promised, but all he received was a promise that they were coming, without any firm arrival date.

John was sitting in the operations room at Kallang aerodrome, reviewing the charts that showed the layout of Royal Air Force stations throughout Malaya. He wanted to ensure he had a working knowledge of all those airfield facilities in case the squadron had to relocate north, to meet any Japanese threat if their forces come down out of Indochina.

There was a knock at the door and the orderly came in. 'RAF Headquarters on the line for you, sir,' he said.

John thanked him and reached for the telephone on his desk. 'Squadron Leader Noble speaking.'

'Squadron Leader, this is Curtis, OC war planning here at HQ. I am calling to advise that a state of emergency, covering Singapore and the Malay Peninsula, has been declared. The view is that the Japanese could launch some sort of attack at any time.'

John was not surprised. Something like this had been expected for the last few weeks, as pressure between the West, led by the US, and Japan, had continued to grow.

'Consequently, your squadron is to go on a war footing, effective immediately.'

'Yes, sir. I will put that in place.'

'Very good. To be clear, this is preparatory only. While there has been no declaration of war by anyone, we do think Japan may be up to something. Notwithstanding that we are effectively moving to full readiness for any conflict that may emerge, there is no suggestion of us undertaking any actual war operations at this time. But we do need to keep a good lookout, so we want Forty-Eight Squadron to run regular patrols to cover the southeastern approaches, and the seas to the northeast, up as far as Kuantan. Right, I must go. We will keep you advised of any developments.'

As John replaced the receiver, he thought about the steps he needed to take. He began by bringing Richard and Don into his office.

'Well, it's not really a surprise, is it?' Richard said, once he had heard what had happened.

'No, it's not, and this is what we will do. First, establish a dispersal area for our aircraft. I don't want them sitting in a line or clustered together. I appreciate we are not at war with Japan, but I want to be prepared in case there should be a surprise attack. HQ seem to think we are impregnable here in Singapore, so it's precautionary only from their perspective. I don't share their confidence. If the Japanese go to war, Singapore would be a valuable prize and they could strike with little warning. Flying Officer Salt, could you get the dispersal arrangements underway, please, as soon as we finish here.

Second, we need to roster reconnaissance patrols. How many aircraft are airworthy at present?'

'Twelve, as of last evening,' Richard answered.

'All right, to ensure we have as many patrols as possible each day to give us good coverage in our reconnoitring, we will operate two-ship flights, starting at dawn, and continuing through to dusk. That should enable us to keep an eye on the eastern approaches to the peninsula, from here up as far as Kuantan, as well as the southeastern approaches to Singapore. Flight Lieutenant Stark, will you establish the precise area for each patrol, based on that, and allocate aircraft and pilots? The objective is to maintain a comprehensive lookout for any Japanese activity, but, of course, there is to be no engagement. We aren't at war yet,' John concluded with a grimace.

'How far off the coast do we go, sir? I'm thinking one hundred and fifty miles.'

'I agree — plan on that basis. That's all for the moment. Let's meet back here at fourteen hundred. Thank you.'

After Richard and Don had left, John walked over to the nearby hut from which the security officer operated.

'If you don't already know, Flying Officer, we are at state of emergency. Declared this morning. Concern about what the Japanese might do.'

'I've heard about it, sir. We have put gunnery on watch, so AA is available should it become necessary. I'm also putting some sentries around the aerodrome. Twenty-four hours a day.'

'I think we also need entry controls at the main gate. Until now, civilians working on the station have just come and gone as they pleased. That's too loose in current circumstances. Can you organise something there too, please?'

'Already addressed that, sir. We are establishing a register of workers, noting their roles, and issuing passes showing their personal detail and what they do here.'

'Good work. I will leave you to it, Flying Officer. Any issues, contact me at the admin office,' John said as he turned to leave.

'Had a call from RAF HQ in the city, sir,' Richard said when John got back to the administration office. 'They were checking we had been advised of the emergency setting. When I confirmed we had indeed been notified, I was asked what arrangements we had put in place. Turns out our patrol arrangements are not acceptable.'

'Why not?' John demanded.

'The officer I was talking to said patrols by two aircraft would have insufficient offensive capability. He said we should operate as a full squadron.'

'Oh, for Christ's sake!' John exploded. 'We aren't even at war. What does he expect us to do if we see Japanese ships or aircraft — attack them?'

'I agree, sir, but I didn't think it was my place to disagree with him.'

'Of course, no problem, Flight Lieutenant. Who was it? I will call him.'

'A Wing Commander Terence Stock.'

'Have you met him before?'

'No, I haven't met him, sir, but I have heard from a colleague who is at HQ that Wing Commander Stock, despite having no operational experience in any war zone, thinks he knows more than the squadron commanders. That was confirmed when he told me he was seasoned in all matters Southeast Asian, and after five years in Singapore was best placed to assess risks and recommend a response to the Japanese threat.'

Five minutes later, John was speaking to Wing Commander Stock on the phone. He had come out of a meeting to take John's call, and was not pleased when he discovered John only wanted to talk to him about something he had raised earlier with the RNZAF squadron at Kallang aerodrome.

'Squadron Leader,' Stock said to John, 'I've made my decision. In my assessment, two-aircraft patrols won't cut it. That's why I told your man your patrols should be undertaken by at least twelve aircraft. The smaller flight of two wouldn't have any real offensive capability.'

John was furious. Did this man have any idea about frontline aerial operations, let alone whether the military was free to act offensively just because a state of emergency had been declared?

'Two things, sir,' John said, trying to keep the anger out of his voice. 'First, I want to operate patrols of two aircraft each, to ensure I have sufficient capability to maintain a continuous lookout for any Japanese presence, air or sea. My squadron has only twelve serviceable aircraft. If I operate full squadron patrols, my reconnaissance ability is severely depleted. Maybe three patrols a day, maximum. I want to undertake multiple sweeps by two aircraft, rather than fewer sweeps utilising the whole squadron. I have two large areas to cover, east of the Malay Peninsula, and the southeastern approaches to Singapore. Twelve aircraft up on a patrol together means we only undertake one sweep in one sector before the aircraft are back for refuelling. I would only be able to patrol each area once a day if following that protocol. That would mean unacceptable gaps in coverage. I can be a lot more effective if reconnoitring using two aircraft on each occasion. Multiple daily patrols in the areas to be covered would then be possible. I don't need the whole squadron up. Offensive capability is not required at present — it's just reconnaissance.'

'That's all very well, Squadron Leader, but what happens if you run into a crowd of Japanese?'

'Well, we might, but we are operating only in a state of emergency. No war has been declared, so offensive ops don't even come into the picture. It's only about reconnaissance at this stage.'

'I know that, Squadron Leader, but it would be good to let the Japanese see us there in force, eh? Might make them think twice about getting restless.'

'In my opinion, whether the Japanese see two RAF aircraft or twelve, that's not going to have any material effect.' As he spoke, John was also thinking the Japanese would have no concern about their ability to take them on if all they saw were obsolete Brewster Buffalos.

Stock started to say something, but John kept talking, cutting across the interruption.

'My second point is more basic. We are in a state of emergency and Command is seeking information, not involvement in any offensive encounter. As I said, we are not at war. The arrangements I have established are the best way to achieve the outcomes currently sought. There is no reason at all in my opinion for patrols to utilise more aircraft — in fact, quite the opposite. There are reasons why we shouldn't, as I've outlined.'

There was a moment of silence before Stock spoke again. 'Do as you wish, Squadron Leader. I have made my point, and you have rejected it. We will leave it at that. Goodbye.'

When Stock hung up, John continued to seethe, then got up and went next door into the operations room, where he found Richard.

'I've spoken to HQ,' he said. 'It will be two-ship patrols, as we discussed. We will aim for three sorties a day in each patrol area, staged evenly throughout the hours of daylight, with the last finishing at dusk.'

Richard grinned broadly. 'Good on you, boss,' he said.

Early the next day, John, accompanied by Owen Gilks, the first member of the squadron he had met when he had arrived at Singapore's Seletar flying-boat base after his journey from Cairo, took off and turned to the northeast. They were to patrol the seas to the east of the Malay peninsula.

Crossing the coast at Desaru as they climbed through fourteen thousand feet, bound for their agreed patrol height of seventeen thousand feet, John checked the time. O-seven-thirty-eight. He calculated they would reach their patrol limit, one hundred and fifty miles off the coast, in forty-five minutes.

The two aircraft were maintaining a higher airspeed than normal for their climb. That was to help protect against the problem Buffalos had been having with overheating engines. The increased airflow resulting from the higher speed helped with cooling. While their additional speed today did mean a reduced rate of climb, there was no urgency to get to altitude. *How different it will be if we end up going to war in these machines*, John thought, looking around his cockpit. Then they would have no choice. Maximum climb rate to altitude would be necessary, to enable them to get to a height at which they could more effectively engage enemy aircraft.

It was a nice day. The sky was cloudless. John settled back in his seat as they climbed and began scanning left to right, looking for any signs of activity on the ocean below, or in the air ahead. Owen Gilks was flying a right echelon station, one hundred yards out from John, far enough away to scan the patrol area himself, rather than having to focus on maintaining his position relative to his flight leader. After forty-five minutes, flying a heading that had taken them straight out to sea from the Malayan coastline, John calculated they must have reached the point where they were about one hundred and fifty miles from shore. That was the limit he had established for their patrols.

'Turning left ninety,' he called, as he banked to a northerly heading, parallel to the now invisible Malay Peninsula. Owen followed.

So far, they had seen nothing of interest — just some fishing boats and a solitary freighter on a course inbound to Singapore. The sea was largely deserted. John was surprised. He had always thought of the ocean around Singapore as comprising busy sea-lanes, with plenty of shipping coming and going. He wondered if the threat of war had persuaded shippers and owners to avoid the area at present.

The patrol had turned north at 0823 hours, so John knew they would be abeam Kuantan, the line of the northern limit of their patrol area in an hour, at 0923. They droned on, continuing their scan of sea and air. Nothing was seen.

'I estimate we are abeam Kuantan, this time,' John called on his radio an hour later. 'Turning left ninety,' he said as he rolled his aircraft into a shallow bank. 'We'll see the coast soon, as we get closer. Forty-five minutes to Kuantan.'

Twenty minutes later, John suddenly sat upright. The regular throb of the engine had seemed momentarily interrupted. He wondered if he had imagined it — easy to do in a single-engine aircraft a long way from land over shark-infested waters.

Then it happened again. Yes, that was a miss. What was happening? Temps and pressures were in the green. The power setting had not been touched. Then John saw his fuel pressure indicator wavering, suggesting fuel starvation. But what was causing it? Vapour lock? Fuel pump failure?

The engine missed again. John grasped the handle of the fuel system wobble pump, working it furiously to build fuel pressure. *That seems to have rectified things*, he decided, as his engine settled into a normal rhythm and the fuel pressure stabilised. *Damn vapour lock — it must have been that. I'll reduce altitude. That will help.*

'Patrol Two, I've been having vaporisation issues,' John called. 'I seem to have got through it. I hand-pumped some fuel, but to reduce the risk of a recurrence I'm going to lose some height. Descending now, to ten thousand. Follow me down.'

'Wilco, Patrol Leader,' Owen responded, reducing power and pitching his aircraft's nose down to follow John's descent.

There was no further fuel problem, but John was nevertheless very pleased to see the Malay Peninsula appear a short time later.

That evening, back at RAF Kallang, John met with Richard to discuss the operations the squadron had undertaken during the day. Five patrols had been flown: two in the area John had covered first thing that morning, and three over the southeastern approaches. Nothing of significance had been seen anywhere. The sixth patrol had not operated, as the aircraft had serviceability issues.

'Reliability is going to be a big factor for us, I suspect, now we are making increased operational demands on the aircraft,' John said.

'Yes,' Richard replied. 'Apart from aircraft grounded for maintenance, we had an instance of an engine overheating. Flying Officer Gilbert was getting undue temperature and oil pressure indications on his climb. He didn't turn back, though. Instead, he stopped climbing and flew level for fifteen minutes or so, and that had it looking healthier.'

'I think as a matter of operational practice, we will climb at a higher airspeed than the Pilot Notes suggest. I did that this morning, when I was out with Flying Officer Gilks, and the increased airspeed seemed to keep the overheating issue under control. It does mean it takes longer to get to altitude, of course, but that's okay on a patrol sortie. It's not a course of action that will be available to us if we move into war operations. Then height, and getting up there quickly, will be important.'

'I agree,' Richard said, 'so the sooner the Hurricanes arrive, the better.'

'Yes, I know,' John acknowledged with a sigh. 'We just have to do the best we can with the Buffalos. Patrols will be fine. We know what to watch out for on the aircraft and can take some steps to mitigate our problems with them. But it's going to be a long way below optimum if we have to fly them in battle against something like the Japanese Zeros. We will need to push our aircraft then, and I'm not confident about their performance.'

CHAPTER EIGHT

John's squadron continued to carry out regular patrols over its designated surveillance areas as December began. Despite some further aircraft serviceability issues, most of the squadron's patrols were able to be completed as scheduled, although some afternoon flying was affected by increasing thunderstorm activity. Singapore was into high summer, something the rainy season now signalled. When a storm formed, patrols would be suspended. No-one could fly until it had passed; conditions in the air were just too dangerous. During those times the pilots would sit in the ready room, trying to cope with their discomfort as they perspired in the high humidity. John had noticed he was losing weight in the tropical climate. *I'm sweating it off*, he decided.

On the afternoon of the seventh of December, yet another thunderstorm was raging over Singapore, and all flying was on hold.

'Bit wet out there,' Richard commented as he and John stood on the operation room's veranda, surveying the scene. Torrential rain was pouring down, and the ground soon became covered in an inch of water. It was pooling faster than it could disperse.

'Atrocious. Couldn't fly safely in that,' John confirmed.

'I see the *Prince of Wales* battle group has arrived, including, besides the *Prince of Wales* itself, the *Repulse*, and four or five destroyers.'

'Churchill is determined Singapore is to be well-protected against any Japanese aggression, so that's a welcome addition to our capabilities here,' John responded.

'If we just had our Hurricanes, sir…'

'Indeed, that would make me feel a lot more comfortable sending the lads up to meet the Japanese, as will be required very soon, I'm guessing.'

They had all seen the newspaper stories about US ultimatums to the Japanese, and no-one expected the Empire of Japan to back down. Just then, there was a roar of laughter from inside. John glanced through the open window. Flying Officer Trevor Roberts had clearly had a good win at the card game six of the pilots were playing. John did not know what the game was, but it clearly excited them, given the ruckus the players were making.

John looked at his watch; it was four-fifty. *This storm has put an end to any more patrolling today*, he decided. Sunset would be in forty minutes, at around five-thirty. There was not enough time to complete the usual flights.

'Flight Lieutenant,' John said to Richard, 'we will cancel the last patrol of each area for now. The storm's gone on longer than expected, and there's not enough time left before dusk. Tell those involved, please. We'll recommence at first light. It's important we get out there early. The Aussies spotted two Japanese convoys yesterday; one appeared to be heading towards the Gulf of Siam, the other towards the Malay Peninsula, northern end. There's something going on.'

That night, John was woken by the sound of explosions in the distance and multiple heavy aero engines. *Christ, it's a bombing raid*, he realised with a start. He groped around in the dark for his clothes and boots. He had decided not to switch on any lights.

Once outside, he saw Richard and Don, who had obviously quickly pulled on some clothes to go out and see what was happening. Moments later, Trevor Roberts appeared, followed closely by Jock Gilbert and Owen Gilks. They all stood watching in silence. They could only hear the aircraft that were bombing, not see them. The explosions to their north and northwest were huge, lighting up the sky with their flashes.

'Why are all the lights in the city on?' John asked. 'We're in a state of emergency, upgraded to level one readiness after those conveys were seen yesterday, but there's no blackout.'

'Aircraft seem to be moving away, northeast by the sound of them,' Jock volunteered.

'I'll call the duty officer at HQ,' John responded, 'and see if we can get some understanding of what's happening.'

Five minutes later, he was on the phone and receiving very unwelcome news from Headquarters. 'Yes, Squadron Leader, I can tell you what's going on,' said the duty officer. 'The Japanese have just bombed Singapore Island. Seletar and Tengah were their targets, and we have been advised that Japanese forces are coming ashore up the Malayan Peninsula, at Kota Bharu.'

'All the lights were on around the town,' John replied. 'Wasn't there any warning from radar that could have given time for a blackout?'

'Radar saw them coming and gave a warning, but it didn't reach the right people in time. Anyway, that's the past. Now, we need to be ready to mount interceptions when they come back. Have your squadron at instant readiness by dawn, please, Squadron Leader. There will be an update as soon as we have the detail, but I can tell you there are reports coming in of a major early-morning attack on Pearl Harbor in Hawaii, overnight our time.'

Oh my God, thought John. *The Japanese have moved to take out the ability of the US navy to intervene in the Pacific.*

*

At first light, six Buffalos from John's squadron were airborne off Kallang, to patrol the immediate vicinity of Singapore Island, in case any more Japanese aircraft were approaching. After ninety minutes, they landed back at the aerodrome and the next six aircraft took off on defensive patrol in the same area. At this stage it was a matter of 48 Squadron providing as much defensive capability as it could to protect Singapore, in case of any further bombing attacks, so the patrols were six aircraft each, and not flying far from base. That ensured continuous cover, as best they could.

Later that morning a formal notice was received from RAF Southeast Asian Command: *Squadrons are to maintain defensive cover, with patrols over the aerodromes we control in Malaya, including Singapore, to operate through daylight hours. Further information/requirements will follow tomorrow.*

John was aware Japanese forces had now taken the airfield at Kota Bharu. Two others, Alor Star and Kuantan, were under attack. He enquired with Command if there was any plan to use his aircraft to help counter the Japanese ground forces mounting the attacks in Malaya.

'No, you are not required to undertake any action against ground positions further up the Peninsula at this point, Squadron Leader. HQ wants to take its time formulating a response, to ensure we get the best result. The invading forces will find their movement difficult, given the impediment to ground transport the jungle provides. That gives the army the opportunity to meet them in due course on the few road routes available, where we can create choke points.'

John said nothing but was dismayed at the apparent lack of planning. The Japanese threat had been around for months, and those controlling British forces were only now developing defensive strategy and tactics?

'Fighter aircraft should maintain local patrols in the interim,' his contact at Command told him. 'The navy is putting the *Prince of Wales* battle group to sea. That group will sail to the area where there are numerous Japanese vessels supporting the landings at Kota Bharu and engage. Preliminary reports from Hawaii indicate a lot of vessels in the US fleet have been severely damaged, and loss of life is considerable.'

If there was any doubt about the intentions of the Empire of Japan, they are now well and truly dispelled, John thought, as the officer from Command continued.

'This is total war, and it appears to be occurring on multiple fronts. As well as Hawaii, and the landings here in Malaya, we are getting reports of the Japanese attacking Wake, Guam, and the Philippines. I will speak with you again soon, when we have more developed plans. At this time all I can say is stay alert, and I wish you the best in any encounter you may have with the enemy.'

John and his squadron saw no sign of any Japanese aircraft during their patrols, but early in the morning of the second day, John received orders to prepare to provide air cover to some warships. The squadron was scrambled shortly after that, with instructions to assist ships of the *Prince of Wales* and *Repulse* battle group. They were being attacked by Japanese aircraft, approximately one hundred and sixty miles from Singapore, off the east coast of the Malay Peninsula.

There was little talk as nine Buffalos climbed steadily to the northeast after take-off. There were only nine because the others were grounded due to serviceability issues. Fifty minutes later, they arrived over the position where the attack had been reported to have occurred. As they circled there was no sign of *Prince of Wales* or *Repulse*, but two destroyers were moving slowly about the area.

'Flight, stay at altitude, and keep watch for hostile aircraft. I'm going to descend to see what I can,' John called, as he throttled back and rolled into a shallow dive, but away from the destroyers, not towards them. If the vessels had been subjected to recent attacks by Japanese aircraft, he knew there may be some trigger-happy gunners on board.

On reaching one thousand feet, John flew slowly past one of the destroyers, at about a mile. He was close enough for them to see he was British, but far enough away not to appear threatening. He saw a light signal near the bridge flash some message in his direction, but he could not understand morse, so had no idea what it meant. The only thing it did clarify was that the warship clearly did not see him as an enemy aircraft.

He circled closer. Looking down, he could see the destroyer was picking people out of oil-covered water. He realised immediately why they had only seen destroyers on arrival overhead. The *Prince of Wales* and the *Repulse* must have been sunk. It was probably their crews being plucked from the water, he decided. He could not confirm that with the vessels below, because the Buffalo's radio did not have the frequency the Royal Navy used. John flew closely past the destroyer and slowly rocked his wings, signalling he had seen what had happened. Then he applied power and began climbing back to where the patrol aircraft continued to circle.

'Flight, this is Patrol Leader. The Navy has lost some ships and they are rescuing survivors. We will hold overhead to provide air cover in case the enemy return.'

No-one said anything, but they all recognised the disaster the Royal Navy had suffered today. Two capital ships, intended to intimidate and dominate the Japanese forces in the area, had been sunk on their first encounter. The Empire of Japan was looking unstoppable. First they had achieved the destruction of the US fleet at Pearl Harbor, then they had successfully landed in Malaya, and now they had sunk the best ships Britain had in Southeast Asia.

After about forty minutes, the destroyers' rescue mission looked to be complete. They were steaming southwest, towards Singapore, at high speed, clearly keen to vacate the area as soon as possible in case the Japanese returned. John called for the squadron to return to Kallang.

When back on the ground, the pilots began their usual duty of reporting on their mission to the intelligence officer, telling him what they had seen as they patrolled over the area where the battle group had suffered the Japanese attack. It was not good news, and they all felt badly affected by what they had seen. The loss of the *Prince of Wales* and the *Repulse* was a catastrophe. John was conscious that even if the attack on the *Prince of Wales* battle group, as it steamed along the Malay coast, had not been over by the time his squadron had reached the scene, the outcome may not have been any different. British Buffalo aircraft were always going to be ineffective against the more capable aircraft being flown by Japanese pilots. The Royal Navy had reported that more than forty aircraft had been attacking them, including covering fighter aircraft.

Over the following days, aircraft from the squadron were scrambled on several occasions to intercept single Japanese aircraft seen off the coast, to the northeast, but otherwise there was little enemy air activity near Singapore. Usually, it was just two Buffalos that went up to chase a single reconnaissance aircraft. John had ruled out sending more than that for the interception of a lone aircraft. Two were adequate to get the job done, and he wanted to ensure there were as many aircraft as possible remaining available at short notice. He expected the Japanese bombers overhead again at any time.

The inadequacy of the Buffalos was again highlighted during this period. When a single enemy aircraft was observed reconnoitring the area, and two aircraft were scrambled to intercept, they were usually unable to get anywhere near their intended target. The Buffalos did not have the performance to climb quickly to the altitude necessary to intercept.

'No luck, I'm afraid, sir,' Richard reported to John when asked about the latest interception attempt. 'The lads just couldn't get close. Their rate of climb, especially in these tropical conditions, is inadequate. Flying Officer Roberts was so frustrated he tried to push his aircraft a bit harder, but ended up having to abandon the chase when his engine overheated and risked failing.'

'I know, I know,' John sighed, wondering when they would have the equipment necessary to allow them some success.

The Japanese air attacks that John expected did not come to pass over the rest of December, which surprised him, but he was happy to have been wrong. He was able to use that time to continue working on the squadron's air combat skills, particularly for the last of those pilots who had needed more training to get up to a standard that would give them a better chance in the air.

In early January, enemy raids targeting Singapore began. John was airborne early one morning, leading a flight of ten Buffalos to intercept inbound Japanese aircraft. It was the first of the raids he had expected to begin some time ago. Climbing through eleven thousand feet, over Johor, John saw the approaching enemy aircraft. Thirty plus, he estimated, and just fighters. No bombers.

'Patrol, this is Leader. Thirty plus hostiles at one o'clock. About two thousand above us,' John called.

John's aerial warfare experience told him this was a very difficult situation. His flight was outnumbered three to one, suffered a height disadvantage, being two thousand feet lower than the Japanese, and the rapidly approaching aircraft were Zeros, a much more capable fighter than the Buffalo.

'Full-power climb; one-thirty air speed for maximum rate; adjust heading forty degrees to starboard,' John called as he made the necessary inputs to his own aircraft. He was trying to position the flight towards a point where the sun would be behind them, making it more difficult for the Japanese pilots to see them. As he watched, John saw the approaching fighters roll slightly left and dive towards them.

'Here they come,' he called bracingly. 'Engage at will.'

Moments later the sky was full of whirling aircraft, as they climbed and turned in multiple dogfights.

John saw Trevor Roberts haul his aircraft into a tight turn to follow a Zero that had just flashed over him after firing a long burst at his Buffalo. As Trevor turned to follow the Zero, John saw another Japanese fighter coming up behind Trevor's aircraft. He called a warning on the radio, but he was too late. John could only watch as the Buffalo took multiple hits and its nose dropped sharply.

'Jump man, jump!' he shouted into his radio as Trevor plummeted down. As he said that, his own aircraft was hit by a hail of fire, its fuselage taking multiple rounds just behind his cockpit. The roar was deafening as his aircraft bucked under the impact. John turned steeply to the left, but his attacker stayed close on his tail. He could not make the Buffalo turn tightly enough to get away, and tracer fire continued to slice past him on each side of his cockpit. He banked hard to the right, planning to roll through two hundred and seventy degrees, then enter a steep turn to the left again, followed by a roll to the inverted position and a pull through into a vertical dive. Halfway through his initial roll, he realised his aircraft was moving too slowly through the manoeuvre. It was nothing like the quick and precise changes of direction and aircraft attitude he had been able to make in his Spitfire, with its fast rate of roll and nimble performance. The lumbering Buffalo was no sprite, and his moves were easily anticipated by the chasing Zero. A burst of fire struck his engine, which stopped almost immediately.

John was in a steep dive, with no power and little control. He reached up and opened the cockpit latch, pushing the canopy back. He hated the thought, but he was going to have to bale out. The wind was strong, despite the sheltering effect of the front windscreen. He struggled to undo his harness in the mayhem. When he was free of his straps, and after ensuring he had located the pull handle that would release his parachute when he was ready, John took his feet off the rudder pedals and positioned his legs back towards his seat. Then he simply stood up, pushing down hard as he straightened his legs to help eject himself from the cockpit. He did not pull the parachute release handle quite yet, knowing he would risk a snag if his chute was out before he was well clear of the aircraft.

Moments later John had stopped tumbling through the air, battered by the furious wind, and was gently swaying as he quietly floated down under his parachute canopy. Looking down, he could see he was descending into a relatively open area on the edge of the rainforest. There were some huts there, and people on the ground who were looking up at him, including three or four children running around and gesticulating wildly in his direction. He could hear them shouting with excitement as he got lower. Despite his circumstances, John allowed himself a smile.

When he reached the ground, an old man greeted him. He appeared to be in charge of the various locals clustered behind him, all peering at John. Some kept glancing towards the thick, black, oil-fired smoke coming up through the forest foliage about half a mile away. The remains of John's aircraft were there, burning furiously.

'My son, he ride bicycle to tell the army men where you are,' said the old man.

'Thank you,' John said. 'How far is it to where the army is?'

'Ten minute by bicycle.'

'Do you have a telephone?'

'No telephone. My son will get people for you,' the old man assured him.

A woman with long dark hair, almost down to her waist, emerged from the closest hut. She was about forty, John guessed, and very slim and petite. She was carrying a cup of black tea.

'Yes?' she asked, proffering the cup.

John thanked her and took it. It was just what he wanted right now. He sat on an adjacent log and sipped away, looking around at the smiling faces of his new friends. *They probably don't have any idea what they may be facing if the Japanese take over here*, John thought sadly. There was little talk. The old man had some halting English, but any deeper conversation was difficult.

After twenty minutes, John heard an engine. Soon, a light truck appeared on the narrow mud road that emerged from the trees about one hundred yards from where he was sitting. When the truck reached the huts, it stopped and two British soldiers got out. They were carrying their rifles, and they were levelled towards John. John stood and walked towards them, wondering why the weapons were being held at the ready.

After a moment, the soldiers slung their rifles over their shoulders.

'I'm pleased to see you,' John said.

'And we are pleased to see who you are,' the leading soldier responded. 'We are part of the garrison at Mersing, but established as a checkpoint on the road about three miles from here. Sorry about our rifles — we weren't sure if we were here to arrest a Japanese pilot or to help a British pilot. Your messenger couldn't give us that detail — just that a pilot had floated in after his aircraft had crashed.'

'I understand,' John replied, before turning to the old man. 'Goodbye, and thank you for the tea and getting the army here.'

The man shook John's hand vigorously, continually nodding and smiling at him as he did so.

'Jump in, sir, and we will take you back to our position. We can organise a ride back to your base from there,' said the leading soldier.

'Thanks. I'm at Kallang, southern side of the island,' John replied.

'Very good. Hang on, sir — the track's a bit rough. Roads here are bad generally. Between the poor roads and the dense rainforest, I don't think the Japanese will be able to make much progress from where they landed, at Kota Bharu. That's certainly the view of the officer commanding British forces. He says it means Singapore is probably safe. I hope he's right.'

CHAPTER NINE

When he got back to Kallang a few hours later, John immediately sought out Richard, who was very pleased to see that his commanding officer had survived.

'Wonderful that you're okay, sir. I wasn't certain what had happened to you. I saw you starting to go down but couldn't watch for a parachute — the Japanese were all over me.'

'Thank you. What's the outcome of the encounter?'

'Not good, I'm afraid. We lost three aircraft, including yours. Flying Officer Gilks has been killed, and Flying Officer Roberts is missing.'

John closed his eyes and pictured Owen Gilks, the cheery young man who had picked him up when he had arrived in Singapore. He was the person who had first alerted John to the hopelessness of the Buffalos — prescient words from a young pilot about to be thrust into war in that aircraft. John thought of Trevor Roberts, too — the unmarried mountain climber who had laughed uproariously as he had played cards just a few nights ago.

John felt a deep despair at the disorganisation of the British air defence in Singapore. In his view, the competence of those charged with defence planning was seriously in question. At least in Britain pilots had a fair chance in their Spitfires, and there were good operational systems available. By the time the much-needed Hurricanes arrived in Singapore, it might be too late.

Two days later, Trevor was found dead, hanging from a tree in his parachute near the wreckage of his Buffalo. But John and the men he was leading were given very little time to mourn. Over the next few days, the squadron took to the air every day to meet enemy aircraft intent on bombing Singapore. The Japanese were relentless, and the squadron's losses quickly mounted as the intensity and number of attacks grew. John's concerns about poor operational systems and his pilots having to fly sub-standard aircraft were vindicated. Following the loss of Owen and Trevor, Jock Gilbert, who had planned to become a doctor, was also killed. His aircraft had caught fire and crashed during an encounter involving over twenty Japanese fighters.

Angry and saddened, John blamed the losses squarely on those managing Singapore's defence. He decided to once again chase Headquarters regarding the promised Hurricanes.

'Ah, I was going to call you today, Squadron Leader,' said the RAF liaison officer who answered his call. 'We've just had a signal. The first Hurricanes should be available at the end of the month. There are thirty coming, and your squadron is getting nine of them initially.'

John was pleased. Finally, an arrival date for the much-needed fighters. 'Thank you. I'm very pleased to hear that. We're struggling against the Japanese Zeros.'

'Squadron Leader, could I caution you about sounding defeatist? That's not what should be being said.'

John hung up without another word. If he had stayed on the line, he may have said something he would regret.

By the third week of January, the continuing losses had reached such a level that the squadron had to combine with another squadron based at Kallang. There were insufficient surviving and airworthy Buffalos to equip two separate operations. John was given charge of the amalgamated squadrons.

'We've had a request to operate a recce mission,' John said to Richard and Don. 'Command wants to know what aircraft are on the aerodrome the Japanese are using at Kuala Lumpur. It's a dicey mission, but I'm happy to take it on, with one other aircraft to act as support.'

'That's going to have you at least a hundred miles behind the current position of the Japanese advance, sir. Is HQ aware of the difficulties that poses, given Japanese air superiority?' Don asked.

'Probably not. They're in denial about the air war. They're certainly not happy to hear any suggestion we're being outflown by better machines appearing in greater numbers, and with more experienced pilots than many of ours. Mind you, they are in denial about most things. The Japanese are advancing rapidly down the Peninsula, often using jungle paths so they bypass any engagement point the army sets up on the roads. Notwithstanding what's happening, the generals still seem to think they have it all under control and the impassable jungle will stop the Japanese coming south.'

'I will come with you, sir,' Richard said.

'I'm happy to join you as well,' Don added.

'Two aircraft only, gentlemen. No sense in risking more. Flying Officer Salt, you come as my number two. Flight Lieutenant Stark, I want you to stay in charge here while I'm out on the mission. I think it's important you do that as my second-in-command.'

'Of course. I understand. When do you plan to go?'

'Early this afternoon. I want to spend some time looking at maps and reports of activity in the area between here and Kuala Lumpur first. We need to take a route that's unlikely to attract attention. I don': want two Buffalos a hundred miles behind enemy lines being confronted by a swarm of Zeros.'

Two hours later, John was taxiing his aircraft for take-off, closely followed by Don in a second Buffalo. They had spent some time planning the reconnaissance mission and had decided to fly along the west coast of the Malay Peninsula on their way to Kuala Lumpur.

'We will stay relatively low, one hundred feet, some four or five miles out to sea,' John had said. 'That will make it less likely that we will be seen than if we are flying higher on a direct track, where enemy troops will be moving about. As we pass the port at Klang, a position we can identify by the small group of islands off the harbour mouth, we will turn inland to Rawang. From there, we run south, towards the surveillance target.'

Airborne, and heading northwest to establish themselves on the agreed track, the two Buffalos were soon flying some miles off the coast. *Hopefully this will work*, John thought. *Unlikely anyone will be peering out to sea with their binoculars.*

Their flight towards Kuala Lumpur was uneventful. After fifty minutes, John could see the group of three or four large islands that marked the entrance to Port Klang. Poor visibility inland, caused by heavy rain showers, prevented him sighting Kuala Lumpur itself, but he knew it was in there somewhere, just out of sight at present with the restricted visibility. He glanced to his left, where Don was about eighty yards out. John gesticulated towards the land, indicating he was turning in, as briefed. Don gave him a thumbs-up. The pilots had agreed not to use their radios to speak to each other unless necessary. They thought radio silence would help them remain undetected.

As they crossed Rawang, John banked to the right and set a heading that would take him directly to the aerodrome being used by the Japanese at Kuala Lumpur. He had climbed slightly to preserve a safe margin above terrain. Don followed. It was hard to navigate accurately, with the poor visibility caused by the passing heavy showers, but John maintained the compass heading he knew should bring them to the aerodrome shortly.

The low cloud and rain were making it hard, John noted, but they also provided useful cover for the aircraft. Suddenly, their target aerodrome was there, just five hundred yards off to the left, and there had been no sign of any enemy activity. Turning towards it, with power slightly reduced to lessen the noise his aircraft was making, John began flying a wide, lazy circle around the aerodrome. There was no response from the ground. No-one shot at them. He could not see any fighters starting up, to give chase.

I don't think they realise we are British aircraft, John thought, when he saw the absence of any reaction. *Two fighters from Singapore are probably the last thing the Japanese expect to be slowly circling around their aerodrome.* He had decided to avoid steep turns and high-power settings, hoping to lull the enemy into thinking the Buffalos were local aircraft. He started a second circuit, busily counting aircraft numbers on the ground and noting their parking disposition. There were at least fifty fighters and around thirty-five bombers.

A puff of black smoke, about fifty yards ahead of him, and the dull *crump* of an explosion signalled to him that the Japanese on the ground had just realised the two aircraft stooging around at relatively low level over the airfield were British. Further puffs of smoke followed as more anti-aircraft shells exploded around them. It was time to go.

John called Don on the radio. 'This is Recce Leader. Let's clear to the south, maximum continuous power. We need to get out of here as fast as we can. I will use clouds as cover where possible. Follow me and keep a lookout for Japanese aircraft.'

'Wilco, Leader.'

As they flew south, John flew close to the banks of low cloud along their route, intending to make it difficult for anyone to see them. They were soon back over Johor, clear of Japanese ground positions. No enemy aircraft had been seen, so they began to relax a little.

Back on the ground at Kallang aerodrome, John contacted Command Headquarters and reported to the army major who had requested the reconnaissance. He was disconcerted by John's report.

'We had no idea they were that well established with bombers in Kuala Lumpur. We thought they were coming out of airfields near the coast southwest of Saigon,' he said. 'This will shake the brass. Thank you, Squadron Leader.'

John was also disconcerted. How could Command, after weeks of aerial attacks on Singapore, not have known the origin of the air raids?

Over subsequent days, the Buffalos based at Kallang were scrambled several times, but no engagements with Japanese aircraft occurred. The enemy either were not where they had been reported to be by the time the squadron got there, or they were much higher than the Buffalos, and unreachable in those aircraft.

At the end of the week, on a rather gloomy Friday, Richard came into the ready hut looking for John.

'Excuse me, sir, Command has an operation for us.'

John and Richard moved into the adjacent planning room to talk, leaving the remaining pilots to exchange questioning looks.

'The army is dug in at Batu Pahat, but is going to have to fall back, otherwise they will be encircled and cut off as the Japanese move through the forest around their flank. HQ is concerned the bridge between there and Kluang may be taken out, to try to trap our troops.'

That worried John. Batu Pahat was only ninety miles from Singapore. The Japanese had come a long way from where they had landed in Kota Bharu at the beginning of the previous month.

'What's the brief?' John asked.

'Command wants us there as soon as possible to engage any aircraft attempting to bomb the bridge. We are to remain on station for as long as we can, or until the army gets everyone across — whichever is first.'

Normally, John would have recommended extended cover by sending two flights separately, with the second taking over air cover when the first flight reached its fuel limits. But that was not possible now. He had only four serviceable aircraft available.

'We will take full fuel to give us just over an hour over the bridge. If we end up engaging, we will need to review that endurance.'

Richard nodded his agreement. It was obvious that the normal consumption rate they used for planning would be thrown out quickly if they became caught up in air-fighting. If maximum continuous power settings were suddenly needed for combat, that rate would go up significantly.

'We will run wide orbits around the bridge — I suggest at eight or nine thousand feet, depending on the cloud. That gives us good height if we see any Vals,' John went on, referring to the Japanese Aichi dive-bombers he knew would probably be used to take out the bridge. 'In fact, we will orbit in two groups. Two aircraft will circle the bridge clockwise, using a three-mile radius. The other two can operate a one-mile radius, but counterclockwise and one thousand feet lower.'

'We're not going to be much of a deterrent, are we, sir? I told Command we only had four serviceable aircraft. The chap I was speaking to said that would have to do, as there were no other aircraft available for this op,' said Richard.

'I agree, Flight Lieutenant — while four Buffalos will be able to provide some level of intervention should enemy bombers turn up, if fighters are there as well it's going to be difficult to defend the bridge. We will do what we can, given that's all we have, apparently. No-one else is available.'

'It's a pity the Hurricanes are still a week away,' Richard said with a sigh.

'They will make a difference, but, in the meantime, we'll do our best to manage,' John responded, trying to inject some positivity.

The four Buffalos had been circling around the bridge they were to protect for about forty minutes when there was a radio call from Richard. He was leading the two-aircraft formation making the wider orbits.

'Zeros, ten plus, diving in on us from the north.'

John, the leader of the other flight, glanced back over his shoulder. He saw them immediately. *They're intent on attacking us. They aren't going for the bridge*, he decided, *otherwise it would be Vals, not Zeros.*

'Engage at will,' John called as he pulled his Buffalo into a steep bank to the left, to turn and face the attackers.

Within moments they were involved with multiple enemy aircraft, dogfighting furiously. Don took a long burst from two Zeros approaching him head-on. He dived under them as they got close, but he was trailing some smoke. John barrel-rolled to try to shake a Zero that had positioned itself behind him and opened fire. He saw the lines of tracer flashing by as he entered a steep turn out of his roll, followed by a diving turn in the opposite direction. His attacker disappeared, but another two Zeros soon latched onto him, and he felt the impact of their fire hitting his aircraft. His Buffalo began slewing left and right. Knowing he could not stay in the air for much longer, John began to make his way back to Kallang. For most of the way, he veered dangerously from side to side.

Once he had landed, he saw the problem. Nearly two thirds of his rudder had been shot away. He was pleased to see Don's aircraft on the ground at the aerodrome, too. The smoke from his engine apparently hadn't resulted in either a fire or a failure, and he had limped in minutes before John. Neither of the other two aircraft had returned, and radio calls to them had gone unanswered.

Thirty minutes later, an orderly informed John that he had a phone call from Headquarters. He went to his office and picked up the receiver warily.

'The Japanese took out the bridge. Where the hell were you?' the army/air force cooperation officer at Headquarters shouted down the line.

'We were there, on station over the bridge, for an hour, until we were attacked by multiple enemy fighters,' John replied curtly. 'They outnumbered us three to one. In the ensuing engagements, two of our aircraft were seriously damaged, but managed to make it back. There were four aircraft on the mission, and the other two still haven't returned. Currently, they are considered missing in action. The Japanese must have sent their Val bombers in after their fighters had either shot us down or forced our return.'

'Four? I asked for your full strength to go up there.'

'Four aircraft is all we have. That is our full strength. Your staff were advised of that when we were first briefed on the mission.'

There was silence from the angry man at Headquarters while he took that in. It was clearly a surprise to him. For John, it was yet another example of the disconnect between some of the commanders involved in the defence of Singapore.

'Very well, you did what you could. I must go. Goodbye.' The line went dead.

John had to stop himself throwing his telephone down, he was so angry.

Don came in, looking grim. 'Reports from the line have two Buffalos being shot down near the bridge, sir. Pilot Officer Tims and Flight Lieutenant Stark are both missing, so we know it's them. Debris has been located at the site where one of the aircraft crashed, but there is no sign of the other aircraft. The pilot was still in the wreck that's been found, but he didn't survive. Identification to follow.'

'Thank you. That is all for now,' John replied quietly.

As soon as Don was out of the room, John collapsed forward in his chair, arms wrapped over his head. Some tears rolled down his cheeks as he grieved the latest losses.

When his telephone rang, he glared at it before picking it up. 'Squadron Leader Noble speaking.'

'Sorry to bother you again so soon,' said the man from Headquarters, 'but this time I have something to say that I think will please you. I've just had a call from a post near Senggarang. They saw an aircraft making a forced landing in a rice paddy. The pilot was uninjured and gave his name as Flight Lieutenant Richard Stark, operating out of RAF Kallang. One of your missing pilots, I presume?'

'That is very good news indeed, sir,' John said, feeling some of the weight he was shouldering lift a little.

'He's on his way back to you now.'

'Thank you for your advice.'

'And another thing, Squadron Leader. Your new Hurricanes will be available for you to uplift from Tengah and Seletar next Tuesday, after thirteen hundred hours. There are five at Tengah and four at Seletar.'

'That is very welcome news. I will arrange collection on Tuesday afternoon. Thank you.'

John hurried out of his office, looking for Don. He was in the planning room, looking anxious.

'Don!' called John when he saw him sitting alone in the room. In his excitement, he forgot to use any formal form of address. 'I've just had a call from HQ. Flight Lieutenant Stark is okay. He made a forced landing near Senggarang.'

'Oh, thank God for that,' Don replied, now smiling broadly.

'And listen to this: our Hurricanes have finally arrived. We're getting nine of them at this stage. They will be ready for collection at Tengah and Seletar next Tuesday.'

'That's good news, sir.'

'It is. Too late, in some ways, but better than never,' John said. He was conscious that the tide would be difficult to turn at this point. The main forces of the Empire of Japan were a mere eighty miles away, with some advance patrols probably closer. At least the squadron would now be able to give a better account of itself when Japanese aircraft approached Singapore.

'How many pilots do we have available currently?'

'Eight, including you, me, and Flight Lieutenant Stark,' Don replied.

'Losing a pilot on today's unsuccessful bridge defence hurts, but at least we're soon going to be able to engage using aircraft that are a substantial advance on the Buffalos,' John said. 'I understand there are thirty Hurricanes arriving, with other squadrons re-equipping as well, so the Japanese may find things a little more difficult for them than they have been to date.'

'Who will collect our new fighters, sir?'

'You, me, and Flight Lieutenant Stark are the more experienced pilots, so we will do it. Three aircraft uplift sorties each. It won't take us long.'

'I can get underway with rating the squadron pilots on the Hurricane quite quickly, sir.'

'Thank you, Flying Officer. We will need to be quick. The defence of Singapore is at a tipping point. The next few weeks will decide the future of the island, and Britain's presence in Southeast Asia for that matter.'

CHAPTER TEN

John climbed up onto the wing of the brand-new Hurricane. It had just been assembled and checked by the maintenance team after its sea voyage from England. Inside the cockpit, he could smell the newness. He was keen to get the aircraft across to Kallang. What a difference these machines would make. John started the engine. He had already undertaken a thorough walk-around inspection, checking the aircraft. The Merlin engine grumbled contentedly as John let it warm up after its first start since post-manufacture testing. Oil temperature and pressure were good. Everything looked fine. John could not wait to get it in the air. This was a considerable step-up from the Buffalo. It was the model that had followed the Mark IIA he had ferried across Africa, but there were only minor differences and he felt comfortable.

After running up the engine and completing the required ground checks, John swung the aircraft around and taxied to take-off position. Soon, he was accelerating along the strip. Lifting off, he felt the Hurricane wanting to climb as its airspeed continued to build. *What a difference from that lumbering brute of a Buffalo*, he thought, smiling as he prepared to land at Kallang after only a few minutes.

By the end of the day, all nine Hurricanes destined for John's squadron had been collected and flown to Kallang. Richard and Don had prepared for their transit flights by studying the Aircraft Manual and Pilot's Handling Notes, and then undertaking some air exercises and circuits. John had also shared with them some practical advice about flying a Hurricane. Their capability and experience showed. Both

Richard and Don were flying the Hurricane competently and confidently within a few hours.

'Flight Lieutenant Stark, I suggest two days to get everyone operational on the Hurricane,' John said when they were all back on the ground. 'Do you think you can meet that? We don't have the luxury of time.'

'I think we can have everyone rated on the Hurricane by the end of the day tomorrow, sir,' Richard responded. 'I propose working through the manual and handling notes as a group tonight, having them think about it overnight, and then sending them off on their first flight in type, probably late tomorrow morning. I'll send them south of the island, where they can practise some manoeuvres and stalling. Then they can come back here for, say, six or seven circuits, and they should be as ready as they will ever be.'

'Sounds as good as it can be, in our circumstances. Proceed on that basis. I will sit in on the groundwork tonight, and I can also help with the pre-flight familiarisation tomorrow.'

Pre-flight familiarisation was a simple but important exercise. A pilot about to undertake his first flight in the Hurricane would sit in the cockpit, ready to go. Someone more familiar with the aircraft would stand on his wing, talking to the pilot about the Hurricane's various nuances in flight, and confirming the position and use of various switches, handles, and levers in the cockpit were understood. It was a useful last input for someone new to the aircraft. After that, the pilot was on his own, using his quickly learnt knowledge of the aircraft and its systems as he carefully flew it through some predetermined routines and completed some landing and take-off circuits. John had no concerns about the process. Certainly, some pilots were better than others, but they were all safe, and the additional flying training undertaken in the Buffalos had left them with a reasonable level of competence.

The next morning, the pilots were all at dispersal at first light. The previous evening's session on the manuals had gone well. The pilots were all well-prepared and had a good grasp of the theory related to Hurricane operation. Now it was time for the practicalities. The first three pilots to go up were each seated in the cockpit of their aircraft. John was on the wing of the first aircraft, Richard, the second, and Don, the third. They were busy, leaning into the respective cockpits and talking with the pilots, ensuring their familiarity with the operating procedures and controls. It took only fifteen minutes, and on completion, those pilots were ready to start and go off to undertake the planned exercises.

After the first three had departed, Richard and Don repeated the wing-briefing process with the remaining two pilots due to go on their initial Hurricane flight. Soon they were away too. All was going well.

'I thought last night's session was good value,' John said to Richard and Don. They were having a cup of tea now their Hurricane initiates were airborne.

'Yes, they were quick to pick up the key features and characteristics of the Hurricane. They've had a lot of operational experience here in recent months, so once it becomes second nature to know what lever or switch to reach for, and the speeds to fly in various flight modes, they will be right on top of the Hurricane,' Richard replied.

Forty minutes later, the first of the Hurricanes returned. Within two hours, all five aircraft were back and circuit training completed. The pilots gathered outside the ready hut, chatting excitedly about what they had discovered while airborne in their new fighters. There was a lot of smiling. They clearly knew this aircraft would make a difference.

'Gentlemen, thank you for your efforts. You are now all cleared for ops in the Hurricane, which I think is going help us a lot against the enemy. So, thank you for your application.'

To John's surprise, the pilots clapped at that comment. *That's a sure sign morale is a lot better than it has been,* he decided.

'HQ has told me they have improved their early-warning capabilities,' he informed the men. 'They now think they will be able to give us more time to get airborne to intercept inbound enemy aircraft, and greater certainty about where they are as they approach Singapore.'

A murmur of approval rippled through the room.

'I have suggested to HQ that we run two-aircraft patrols to help keep a lookout for any enemy air activity. That has been approved, so we start those patrols at first light tomorrow. While two patrol aircraft are up — and I envisage ninety-minute missions — the remaining six aircraft will be on five-minute readiness. It's six aircraft on standby while two patrol because we are limited by having only eight pilots. Our ninth aircraft will be used as a spare if needed, until we get another pilot.'

'The aircraft on five-minute readiness will be available to scramble for any sightings by the airborne patrol, or to any alerts provided by the early-warning system. When a patrol lands, two of the ready aircraft will then undertake the next patrol. Those just completing patrol will be refuelled and join the other aircraft on readiness, and so on, cycling through the day, through all eight of the aircraft. If there is a call to scramble, we will probably launch all Hurricanes, unless it's just to chase a lone reconnaissance aircraft, in which case we will just send one after it. We have too few aircraft to do otherwise.

I don't want to commit a lot unless we are facing a major raid — then we will need everybody.'

Well before dawn the next day, John was woken by an airman.

'Sir, sorry to wake you, but HQ wants you to call them straight away.'

Must be urgent, John thought as he stumbled down the corridor to the telephone at the entrance to the officers' sleeping quarters.

'Squadron Leader Noble, Forty-Eight Squadron CO. I've been asked to call urgently.'

'Stand by, sir. I will find who that was and get him on the line,' the duty operator at Headquarters replied.

After a pause, a new voice came on the line.

'Thank you for calling me, Squadron Leader,' said the officer from HQ who had wanted to speak to John. 'I'm sorry about the hour, but I have been tasked with managing central control over our aerial air-defence capability, and I need to talk to all COs before daylight. We are expecting things to hot up today.'

John made no comment, wondering what was coming.

'First,' the officer continued, 'I understand you have taken on register nine of the new Hurricanes. Correct?'

'Yes, sir. We uplifted them from Tengah and Seletar on Tuesday afternoon, but I'm only able to operate eight of them. I'm short of a pilot.'

'Okay. Are your chaps operational on type now?'

'Yes, we've undertaken an accelerated familiarisation programme, and all of my pilots are rated and ready for operations in the Hurricane.'

'Good. I want you available on instant readiness today.'

Instant readiness? That's not practical, John thought. *The chaps can't sit in their aircraft, waiting, in Singapore's heat and humidity.*

'I had in mind a five-minute readiness, sir. That allows the pilots to sit in the hut, out of the sun, but close enough to be airborne very quickly in the event of a scramble. I was also planning to operate two-aircraft patrols on a regular basis to observe any enemy activity, whether on the ground or in the air.'

'No, Squadron Leader. Patrols are not required, nor do we want you to undertake them.'

'Very well, sir. HQ had indicated approval for the patrols. If that's now changed, I won't run them. The squadron will be ready to go on short notice, but it would be counterproductive to have the pilots in the cockpit in the full sun, on instant readiness. I believe five minutes should be fine.'

'All right, Squadron Leader,' the officer said after a pause. 'I accept waiting in the shade is sufficient. In-cockpit standby may not be sensible in Singapore's climate. We will do it as you suggest, but you need to ensure you can respond quickly to any call to action we make.'

'Certainly, sir,' John replied, hoping the performance of the early warning system was better than it had been in the past.

He made his way to the ready hut and found Richard and Don standing outside. 'Patrols are cancelled,' he told them. 'HQ wants us on five-minute standby to any alert issued when enemy aircraft are detected approaching.'

'Well, I hope they are quicker with their identification of an airborne enemy threat than in the past,' Don noted.

'And more effective in giving us an accurate interception course and height,' added Richard.

'I'm sure it will be fine,' John said, trying to hide his concern. He was not at all sure Command had remedied its failings in detecting and alerting fighters about approaching enemy aircraft. *Let's hope I'm wrong,* he thought.

Around nine-thirty that morning, twelve Japanese bombers thundered in towards RAF Kallang, approaching from the southeast. They had come in over the sea, after following a course down the eastern side of the Malay Peninsula some miles off the coast, keeping low to help avoid detection. John and his squadron were taken by surprise. There had been no warning. The first they knew about the raid was the slowly growing roar of aircraft engines approaching. Don had seen them first, as he had searched the horizon trying to identify the source of the noise. 'Enemy aircraft, bombers, southeast at three miles! Scramble!' he shouted to the other pilots. They all ran for their aircraft.

John was in his aircraft quickly and had started the engine within seconds of easing into his seat. He glanced around to see how the others were getting on. Most had their propellors turning. Some were starting to move forward for take-off. As he buckled his harness, John heard explosions. Looking to the southern end of the airfield, he saw the first wave of enemy bombers was overhead, and bombs were whistling down to the aerodrome's grass surfaces, causing large eruptions of earth when they landed and detonated.

There were no other aircraft in his path, so John pushed his throttle forward to maximum power and charged across the ground. The surface from where he had been parked was completely clear and relatively smooth. He was on the aerodrome's take-off and landing area within seconds, already indicating fifty miles per hour on his air speed indicator. Another seventy-five yards and he was airborne, climbing furiously to attack the bombers that were pounding his airfield.

John saw two Hurricanes to his left, and three more to his right, all climbing to position for attack. *Good*, he thought, *at least six of us have got up without being hit. Wonder how the other two did?* But he had no time to dwell on his question; he was too busy positioning behind a bomber approaching Kallang aerodrome. His Hurricane closed in rapidly on the Japanese attacker. When he was three hundred yards behind, John unleashed a two-second burst of fire. He saw he was hitting the bomber around the area of its right engine. It started smoking and as he watched, the wounded aircraft began to roll to the right, its angle of bank becoming progressively steeper. Then it suddenly plunged earthwards. 'Got you,' John muttered, smiling grimly as he turned to look for his next target. Another bomber was lumbering along out to his left. John swung towards it and began to position himself for a shot. Then there was an urgent radio call.

'Zeros, twenty plus, diving in from the northeast.'

John looked up. Sure enough, there were the reported Japanese fighters. The bombers' protection had arrived. He decided to complete his attack on the aircraft he was chasing before positioning to meet the fighters. Within seconds he was close enough to shoot. A quick burst hit the bomber's tail, which detached from the fuselage as it disintegrated under the impact of his concentrated fire. The Japanese aircraft pitched violently nose-down and plunged earthward.

John wheeled around to face the Zeros. They were now only about two thousand yards away, he thought, and within seconds he was engaged in a dogfight with two of them. He pulled a maximum-rate turn to get in behind one of the Zeros, then fired a quick burst. His tracer floated past the Japanese aircraft as it quickly rolled steeply left and dived away. John did not follow, instead scanning around for another target. His aircraft shuddered as machine gun and cannon fire from one of the Japanese fighters stitched a path across his Hurricane. The holes from the cannon fire were substantial.

Ah, nothing serious hit. I still have control, John thought fleetingly, as he wrestled his aircraft into a series of manoeuvres to escape the attack. He rolled inverted then pulled back hard on his control stick, entering a dive. He levelled his aircraft after losing about one thousand feet of altitude and steep-turned to the left. *Nothing in my cockpit mirror,* he noted, after completing those actions. He scanned over each shoulder, then above and below his aircraft. Just as he decided he must have shaken off his pursuer, his Hurricane was wracked by another salvo of enemy fire that hit around the tail area. *Christ, were did that come from?*

A Japanese aircraft climbed past him, before levelling and rolling into a turn back towards John's Hurricane. It had clearly been under him, in a blind spot. He could feel his elevator control was not working properly. It required full control inputs, forward or back, just to manage a small pitch change. John was head-to-head with the Zero now. He saw the flashes around the Japanese aircraft's guns as it began firing. He fired back. *Who's going to break away first?* John wondered as the two aircraft closed in towards each other. At the last minute, he rolled right and entered a dive. The Zero raced past in an instant, too fast to turn effectively and get onto John's tail.

As John slowly pulled out of his dive, he saw a Japanese bomber heading north, back to its base in Malaya, he guessed. It was a good target of opportunity — directly ahead of him and flying straight and level at a much slower speed than John's aircraft. If the bomber crew were starting to think they were safe, on their way home to base after a successful raid, they were mistaken. John put a long burst into the Japanese aircraft, hitting a fuel tank that exploded with an enormous flash and powerful detonation. The enemy bomber instantly became a flaming mass which fell from the sky so quickly no crew member had time to parachute to safety.

Looking around, John could see no sign of any more Japanese aircraft, so he reduced power and started descending towards Kallang aerodrome. Arriving overhead, he was horrified to see the damage. Buildings were on fire, the airfield was covered in bomb craters, and there were three burnt-out aircraft airframes: two on the dispersal area and one some two hundred yards away, on the airstrip. *Damn, that's a third of my new Hurricanes gone in one attack*, John thought.

Once he had landed, he made his way to the planning room and found Richard.

'Two of our aircraft were destroyed at dispersal. One was the spare,' Richard told him. 'We also lost Pilot Officer Michaels. His aircraft was destroyed by a direct hit while he was taking off.'

John remembered him clearly; he had been a nice young chap, with a mop of ginger hair and a constant smile. 'What other losses?' he asked tensely.

'Nine ground crew were killed in the raid. We've also lost the maintenance hangar and all our tooling that was inside. That's going to make things difficult. The only good news is we shot down two Zeros and five bombers.'

'Better than nothing, but we've paid a high price. A third of our Hurricanes taken out, ten killed, and we've lost our maintenance facilities and equipment.'

'You said HQ had indicated systems for better early warning of Japanese raids were in place, sir. No call to scramble had been made before we saw approaching enemy aircraft today, so that tells me they haven't yet sorted the problem.'

'I agree, Flight Lieutenant,' John replied, 'and I'm going to take it up with Command. If they had let us patrol, as I suggested, we may have been better prepared to meet the enemy and avoid some of the losses we've suffered.'

He hurried into his office and phoned Headquarters. The RAF liaison officer answered.

'Squadron Leader Noble, the decision has been made here that there will be no patrols,' he said. 'The only reason you were caught on the ground at Kallang today was because there was a communication breakdown. That prevented an alert being sent to your ops officer in time. It won't happen again; we have undertaken a further review, and failsafe arrangements have now been put in place.'

John was not confident that what he was hearing was accurate, but he had made his point, demanded better, and had now been told he would get what he wanted in future: adequate warning of inbound attacking aircraft. There was not much more he could do other than make it clear that the failure of the so-called early warning system had cost lives and valuable equipment.

'Satisfactory, sir?' Richard asked John as he emerged from the room where he had made his call.

'They say today's early warning fiasco was caused by a communication breakdown, and that it won't happen again. They better be right.'

CHAPTER ELEVEN

As the sun rose in the east, the first fingers of light over the South China Sea touched the aerodrome at RAF Kallang. John was sitting quietly on the low deck outside the ready hut in his favourite cane chair, looking over the operational area of the airfield. The beauty and stillness of the dawn belied the carnage of burnt-out aircraft hulks, cratered runways, and destroyed buildings. Only six Hurricanes were left after yesterday's early-warning fiasco.

Suddenly, a series of large explosions filled the air. Looking towards the area from where the sound of the blasts was coming, he saw three Japanese bombers approaching. They were bombing the harbour. Behind the three bombers, there were more. Maybe fifteen in total. John was stunned. Not just by the attack, but by the fact that once again the early warning system had failed.

Outraged at yet another system failure, he ran for his aircraft, as other pilots did the same. But John never reached his Hurricane. A line of explosions rippled along the length of the aerodrome towards the dispersal area as bombs fell. His Hurricane was hit and disappeared in a fireball. With no aircraft for him to fly, John changed direction towards one of the slit trenches dug recently to provide some shelter from attack. As he ran, he found himself thinking about the flight sergeant in charge of the digging detail. He had been quite proud of his trenching, though he had warned that they were only good for nearby impacts rather than direct hits.

John jumped into the trench, landing heavily, but the soil at the bottom of the trench was soft and he did not hurt himself.

He lay there, panting and staring at the earth inches from his face.

'No warning again,' a nearby voice called. John lifted his head. Don was lying four or five yards away.

'None. Bloody hopeless,' was John's short reply. As he said that, there was a huge explosion and John's world went black.

John was not sure how long he had been unconscious. It may have been seconds, it could have been minutes, but he was sure of one thing. He was buried under a huge mass of soil and had only a small space around his face and nostrils that appeared clear, allowing him to breath in warm, stuffy air that carried a strong smell of wet earth. He tried to move his arms and legs, but they were pinned. He fought back a wave of claustrophobia, telling himself to be still and to try to relax until help came. It was difficult, but he knew panicking would only make things worse.

Then he felt movement behind his back and realised someone was digging the earth away from around him. Rescuers had obviously arrived, but he was surprised he could not hear much as they worked. A few minutes later, he realised his legs had been uncovered. He could move them backwards and forwards a little. Then earth was being scooped away from around his head, and he could see light as it was removed. A moment later, John was staring at the smiling face of Flight Sergeant Purau, the architect of RAF Kallang's slit trenches.

He said something, but John could not hear him clearly. There seemed to be something wrong with his ears.

An hour later, John was lying on one of the beds in the sick bay, which consisted of a basic wrought iron frame with a kapok mattress.

'Squadron Leader,' the base doctor said as he leaned close and spoke directly into John's right ear, 'you have suffered some loss of hearing as a result of a bomb exploding very close to your trench.'

John could just make out what was being said. He nodded to show he understood.

'We will run some tests before you go, to see what can be done, if anything.'

What if I can't fly again? John thought as his heart started to thump. *And where am I going?*

'Your squadron has no aircraft left,' the doctor continued. 'They were all destroyed in the raid. I'm advised you and the other members of the squadron are to evacuate by ship, to the East Indies. That will occur within the next twenty-four hours. There will be some fresh aircraft waiting for you in the Indies, to re-equip the squadron. You are to help with the defence of Java, based out of Tjililitan, once established there. Some new pilots will be joining you. Your hearing loss means you are grounded at present, so no flying for you until we see what's happened, and its likely effect. As I said, I will organise some preliminary tests before you go.'

John was devasted as he thought about the likely casualties of the latest attack. Then he remembered Don had been near him in the trench before the explosion.

'Flying Officer Salt was in the trench with me. Is he okay?'

The doctor paused. 'No, I'm afraid he's not. His body has been recovered from under the earth that buried him. He suffocated.'

John lay staring at the ceiling, trying to control his grief over Don and his anger towards those commanding the defence of Singapore.

*

The Royal Navy destroyer eased its way out of the harbour, bound for Batavia. Air Force personnel crowded its open decks. There was nothing left to fight with back in Singapore, so the plan was that they evacuate and re-form in the Dutch East Indies. John and various squadron members were near the aft of the vessel's main deck, next to a machine gun installation. It was two days since the explosion had buried John, but thankfully he could sense his hearing was improving. The doctor's tests had indicated that a full recovery was likely within a week.

'Couldn't have got more aboard if they'd tried,' Richard commented to John as he looked around the crowded deck.

'No doubt about that,' John agreed. 'There's not much room to move. Just as well we're only going to be at sea for a few days and the weather's fine.'

'What now?' Richard asked. 'I suppose the Japanese will try to get across the Johor Straits any day. They are shelling targets in the north of the island. Tengah and Seletar are unusable.'

'I've been ordered to re-establish the squadron at Tjililitan. We're going to get some new Hurricanes.'

'Where's that?'

'Virtually part of Batavia itself. We'll have a bit of work to do, re-establishing ourselves as an operational fighter squadron, but I don't see any reason why we can't be operational within a few days of the arrival of fresh pilots and replacement aircraft.'

As he said that, an urgent-sounding klaxon started blaring throughout the ship.

'Action stations, action stations!' a voice called through the destroyer's loudspeaker system. Crewmen, identified by their white T-shirts, the Royal Navy's on-board tropical working kit, were running to establish themselves at their designated positions. John saw the funnel begin to belch thick black smoke. *Someone's stoked up the engine power*, he decided. He took a step to steady himself as the vessel heeled over in a sudden turn. Then he saw a line of Japanese Aichi dive-bombers coming in low over the water, directly towards the ship carrying them to Batavia.

There was a deafening roar as one of the ship's Lewis guns, close to where John was standing, opened up. He saw the arc of tracer dancing towards the leading attacker, but the aircraft kept coming, seemingly unaffected. A hail of bullets clanging into the ship's hull and superstructure caused him to dive onto the surface of the deck, pressing himself as low as he could. The Lewis gun stopped firing. John cautiously looked up. The two sailors who moments ago had been operating the gun, one shooting, one feeding ammunition, were both clearly dead. Their bloodied remains lay slumped against a guard rail.

'With me, Flight Lieutenant!' John called to Richard, picking himself up and moving quickly. Stepping past the sailors' bodies, he was careful not to slip on their blood. *Got to get this going again*, he thought, as he fiddled with the mechanism to realign the Lewis gun's fat barrel — a water device for cooling, he recalled from somewhere. Richard reinserted the beginning of the ammunition feed into the gun and John began firing. He did not realise it at the time, but the oncoming attackers were not only being shot at by the destroyer's light armament, including his Lewis gun, but also by the many soldiers aboard who had unslung their rifles and were taking potshots at the Japanese aircraft. Somebody must have hit one of the pilots, as his aircraft, while showing no anti-aircraft fire damage, suddenly pitched up, hung in the sky for a moment, and then plunged straight down into the grey, oily waters of the harbour.

There was a brief cheer from some, before they continued to fight to survive.

There were explosions all around, and huge eruptions of seawater as bombs hit the surface, but none of the Japanese aircraft managed to hit the destroyer. Then it was over. John could see all the enemy aircraft heading north, back towards the aerodromes they had captured, and were now using, further up the Malay Peninsula.

'That was a close-run thing, but the end for these poor chaps,' John said to Richard as he looked towards the two seaman who had first been operating the Lewis gun.

Royal Navy personnel arrived and quickly removed the bodies, and then another young seaman hosed the area clear. John understood that this was necessary, but he could not help feeling it was a cruel ending for two young sailors, with some of their remains being simply sluiced into a large gutter, and then overboard.

They sailed on and were soon well out into the South China Sea, moving past various small islands to the south of the Singapore Strait. All on board were beginning to feel relatively safe from any further Japanese air attack.

After three days at sea, they berthed at Batavia. John immediately arranged for a car to take him and Richard to the aerodrome at Tjililitan. They were both dismayed to see that little had been organised for the squadron's arrival when they got there. The only good thing was that the aircraft they would use were already on base.

John recognised that he had a substantial task ahead, getting everything set up and established at Tjililitan, particularly training the new pilots he was due to get. He and Richard were the only pilots of the squadron who had survived Singapore.

He grimly surveyed what he had: fifteen Hurricanes that looked like they needed significant work before they could be flown or used on war operations, and only a few of the aeronautical tools needed to allow efficient and effective work on the aircraft. Much of the work necessary would have to be done in the open. There were no hangars for them. He knew the tropical downpours that accompanied the daily thunderstorms here would make that difficult.

In the afternoon, John was summoned to Air Headquarters in the centre of Batavia. He left Richard in charge at the aerodrome and made his way there. When he arrived, he was taken straight to Air Commodore Rogers.

'Welcome to Java, Squadron Leader Noble. I trust you are settling in with your people and finding things as you need them,' said the Air Commodore.

'There are some things I still need, sir, but we will manage, provided my replacement pilots arrive soon. Do you know where they are?'

'No, but they should be with you by the end of the week. We want you and your Hurricanes operational as soon as possible. The Japanese have crossed Johor Strait, on to Singapore Island. We aren't comfortable the garrison will be able to hold out, despite Prime Minister Churchill demanding they resist at all costs. If we are right, and Singapore falls, we expect the invaders will waste little time in launching an attack against us here. Your role is to help with the fighter defence of Batavia. That's going to be critical. Tell me what you need.'

'Well, apart from fresh pilots — only two of us have survived Singapore — I need fuel, aircraft ammunition, and spares. There's little of that at the base at present. Maintenance facilities are difficult, and I can see some of the Hurricanes need some work. Quartering supplies for my squadron is another issue. There is little in the way of bedding and towels. I will make a full list of all our needs and have it sent here as soon as I'm back at Tjililitan. Supply will have to be quick if you are right, and my replacement pilots are just a few days out.'

'Very well, Squadron Leader, I will await your advice and then make sure you get what you need. As I said, the air defence of Batavia is critical, and you and your squadron are planned to be a large part of that.'

As John left Air Headquarters, after a cup of tea that the Air Commodore insisted they have, he felt some unease. Not just because of the Japanese threat, nor because of what he had found, or more accurately, had not found, at his new base, but because there seemed to be no forethought or planning in anything that was happening. *Maybe it's unfolding more rapidly than expected*, John thought.

'Everything okay at HQ, sir?' Richard asked John when he arrived back at the base.

'I've been told we are to be an important cog in Batavia's air defence against the Japanese. The thinking is they will begin offensives against the Indies, soon,' John replied, trying not to sound too dismal about where things seemed to be going. 'Command has asked we submit a list of what we need, and they will organise supply. Could you arrange that, please? I suggest two lists. One around the base's housekeeping needs, the other referencing the squadron's operational needs. And we need to get a training programme ready, so new pilots can be prepared when they arrive.'

'Will do, sir,' Richard responded.

Over the next twenty-four hours John and his ground-team made good progress as they finished setting up and began the many tasks necessary to prepare for aerial operations. The weather was playing its part too. No storms had interfered with work on aircraft, either in the open or under some temporary tent-flies that Richard had procured somewhere. It was late afternoon, and John and Richard were meeting to sign off on the final requests to be made to Air Headquarters, when the telephone rang.

'Squadron Leader Noble,' John said as he answered the call.

'Air Commodore Rogers here, Squadron Leader.'

'Hello, sir, I was just finalising our lists of requirements, if that's what you are calling about.'

'It's not. The garrison at Singapore has just surrendered. Things are moving rapidly.'

Even though John had known the defence of Singapore was not going well, he was surprised by the speed with which the island had been overpowered. He glanced anxiously at Richard but said nothing as the Air Commodore continued.

'The situation has been reviewed. Your squadron is not required to undertake air defence duties. Anyway, I've now been advised that your replacement pilots are not available for some weeks. They're still in New Zealand. No, you are to pack up and sail to Australia. We are not able to set up any air defence capability here in the time available, so you are not required. My staff will be in touch tomorrow with travel orders and passes.'

Embarked on their steamer at Batavia, John was still in shock as he reviewed recent events. The Imperial forces of Japan had landed on the eastern beaches of the Malay Peninsula early in December. Just over two months later, his squadron had been virtually annihilated, forcing an evacuation to the Dutch East Indies. Now, they had been released from the Indies without becoming operational, and were being sent to Australia because they could not be readied in time to meet the oncoming enemy forces.

Complete victory for the Japanese, John thought. He was bitter, unimpressed with the leadership he had seen exhibited by some in Malaya. Lack of effective preparation had cost many lives and had eventually resulted in a humiliating loss for British forces. Aboard the steamer, there was little for John to do but brood over all that had passed.

After nearly two weeks of restricted rations, mostly bully-beef and biscuits, they finally reached Australia. It was good to be out of Southeast Asia, and away from the disorganised military operations they had suffered there, but it was also depressing. John was now wondering whether the Japanese could ever be stopped.

After disembarking in Freemantle, in Western Australia, those who made up what was left of the squadron, mostly ground staff, were transported to a nearby army base.

'Squadron Leader,' the base commander greeted John when he reported to him, 'you and your men are to relocate to New Zealand. You are on a troop train tomorrow, bound for Adelaide, and from there you will take a vessel to Wellington. I have your complement as two officers and twenty-four other ranks. Is that correct? It seems a small number.'

'Yes, sir. That's all we have left.'

The commander paused, an expression of sympathy passing across his face. 'Very well, thank you, Squadron Leader. All the best for your trip to New Zealand. You will be met at Wellington docks and transferred to RNZAF Ohakea. I understand that once there you will be tasked with establishing a new fighter squadron. The RAF has agreed to a request that you be available to complete that, before returning to Great Britain.'

John was surprised he was not going straight back to the United Kingdom, but he decided the role proposed for him on his return to New Zealand would be a welcome change. Quite apart from sharing his extensive war operations experience, and helping prepare young pilots for what they would no doubt soon face in the South Pacific as Japan extended its presence, he could get down south and visit his parents. He had not seen them since leaving the family farm to join the Royal Air Force in 1938.

CHAPTER TWELVE

The day John's ship sailed into Wellington, New Zealand's harbour-capital, it was very windy, with gusts over sixty miles per hour being recorded at the nearby Pencarrow Lighthouse. As his vessel berthed, John could see the ship's crew and the dockworkers were being well and truly tested by the conditions. Continual squalls were hitting the boat, the force often moving it sideways, risking a collision between the ship and the wharf. But the men struggling to safely moor the vessel were obviously used to the wind. Soon, it was securely tied up, and passengers were able to disembark.

After some relatively simple arrival formalities, John was directed to a grey Commer van parked near his vessel's gangway. The van would transfer him to RNZAF Ohakea, the airbase ninety miles north of Wellington, the officer in charge of service arrivals told him. Richard was not going to travel with John. He had been given five days' leave and would rejoin John at Ohakea the following week.

The Commer had been hired by the Royal New Zealand Air Force from a private operator, and the civilian driver talked to John virtually non-stop during the almost two-hour journey.

'Windy, eh?' the driver said as John got into the van. 'Typical for Wellington. Always blowing.'

John smiled his agreement. He was aware of the city's reputation.

'Where have you come from?' the driver continued.

'Sailed from Adelaide. Before that I was in west Australia, having got out of Singapore just before it fell.'

'Bloody hell. You're lucky the Japanese didn't get you. They've been doing terrible things to the locals, and some of our boys too. I tell you, if they come here, they will cop it. You can't do that sort of stuff without being held to account, and they will be.'

'I'm not sure they will get down this far,' John responded, as the driver started another tirade.

'We'll unleash the Māori Battalion on them. The Japanese won't know what's hit them. They're tough, those Māori boys,' he said with a chuckle.

The first thing John did on arrival at RNZAF Ohakea, was telephone his parents. He had tried to call them from Australia but he had not been able to get an international line. If you were senior staff engaged on official business, an international call was possible, but not for a squadron leader wanting to telephone home.

'Dad, it's John. I'm back in New Zealand.'

'John!' his father, Cusack, replied in surprise. 'Good to hear from you. We worried when we saw what happened in Singapore. Glad you got out okay. Your mother's been fretting that the Japanese might have you.'

'No, I'm out and well, thanks. Just arrived at my new base — Ohakea.'

'Will you be in New Zealand for a while?'

'For some months at least. The RAF have seconded me to RNZAF Training, to help prepare the chaps here for the Pacific air-war that's coming.'

'Any chance you could get some leave, and come down to see us?'

'Not sure at this stage, but if I can, I will. Once I know more about my commitments, I'll be in touch.'

'Your mother and I would like to see you. She's down in the village now, and will be disappointed to have missed speaking to you.'

'I will try to arrange something. Must go now. Love to Mother.'

After his phone call, John reported to the commanding officer at Ohakea, Wing Commander David Matthews.

'I am pleased to meet you, Squadron Leader,' said Matthews. 'I've been following how it has been going for you and Forty-Eight Squadron in Singapore. From what I've heard, it's been hard.'

'If I described it as difficult, that would be an understatement, sir. Our aircraft, Brewster Buffalos, were simply not up to any effective combat role. That was compounded by the fact the organisational systems necessary to operate adequate air defence were not in place, or if they were, they certainly didn't operate in any useful way.'

'Yes, I had heard it was all a bit of a debacle. The surrender was a surprise too.'

'It all unfolded very quickly,' John replied. 'The Japanese ground forces came down the Malay Peninsula with speed, despite Malayan Command's view that they would struggle through the rainforest and swamps and be obliged to follow the few main roads. They caught our troops out with the speed of their advance. I heard they were using bicycles on forest paths at one stage, enabling them to bypass and outflank fixed British positions on roads. In the air, they had capable fighters and a range of light bombers. We were outnumbered three to one on most aerial encounters, and that's before even considering the inability of the Buffalo to match their fighter aircraft.'

'Yes, poor show from the leadership by all accounts. However, that's happened, and now we must prepare for the next steps. The push is to get our pilots up to a good operational standard. Our pilots are capable, but they have had no air warfare exposure. I'm pleased to say we do have capable fighters being delivered over coming weeks, so that's a plus. We're getting the Curtiss P Forty Kittyhawk. It comes with an excellent reputation. Getting the chaps up to a good standard in those aircraft is where you come in, Squadron Leader. We've established a new squadron dedicated to advanced fighter training. Presently the squadron has Harvards, but soon they will have the Kittyhawks '

'Who is the CO of the training squadron? I would like to meet him as soon as possible to get a schedule agreed,' John replied.

'You are, Squadron Leader. We want you to take command. You're the ideal person, given your background.'

John was momentarily taken aback. He had not expected to be appointed commanding officer of the new squadron the New Zealanders were establishing, but it was a role he was happy to accept.

John wasted no time in setting up the required training regime, and all was going well when Wing Commander Matthews came to check in with him three weeks later.

'I'm pleased everything is going according to plan, Squadron Leader,' said Matthews. 'The adjutant tells me the training programme is right up to schedule, and we are seeing some good results from the pilots. I understand they have progressed to advanced combat manoeuvring exercises.'

'Yes, they are doing well, sir,' John replied.

'Good. The Kittyhawks will be here next week, and you will be re-equipped immediately after they have been checked and released to service.'

John was delighted. The Harvard was a reliable machine as a two-seat trainer, but it was no fighter. The Kittyhawk would give the squadron a significant lift in capability.

'We do think it likely we will be up in the Pacific taking on the Japanese quite soon,' Matthews continued, 'so the arrival of the new aircraft is timely. Now, as well as confirming the arrival of the Kittyhawks, I wanted to let you know we are going to move your operation to RNZAF Masterton. I won't go into all the reasons for that, but we want you and the squadron at that station as soon as possible.'

Two weeks later, John and his squadron were installed at their new airbase, with twenty Kittyhawks on register. The base was next to the small town of Masterton, from which it took its name. It was situated south of Ohakea, lying on the eastern side of a range of hills known as the Tararuas. Despite not being particularly high hills, when a strong westerly wind blew in from the Tasman Sea, it was enough to kick up some nasty turbulence. One of the squadron's pilots had discovered that after only a few days operating from the new base. Severe turbulence had flung his aircraft around so much he had cracked his head against the cockpit canopy, resulting in a deep laceration.

Most of the pilots referred to RNZAF Masterton as Hood, the name the aerodrome had been given before the war. That name recognised a pilot who was presumed to have died in 1928, attempting to be the first to fly across the Tasman Sea, John discovered. It seemed Mr George Hood had simply vanished on his flight from Australia to New Zealand.

At the end of his second week at Hood aerodrome, John took off early in the morning, flying one of the new P-40 Kittyhawks. He was heading for Wigram, the RNZAF station at Christchurch, where a meeting was planned with Officer Commanding Training John wanted to discuss the pilot training programme there, which took trainees from *ab initio* stage to a basic flying level, all in Tiger Moth aircraft. In John's view, the pilots coming out of Wigram should have skills more aligned to the advanced training they would undertake at RNZAF Masterton. He did not want pilots arriving after completing their basic training in Tiger Moths at Wigram, and then moving straight into air warfare training in the advanced Kittyhawk aircraft.

He thought the gap between flying a Tiger Moth and flying a Kittyhawk was too large, and there had been several near misses. John acknowledged he had gone through something similar during his own training in Britain, moving from a Miles Magister to a Spitfire, but nevertheless, he thought there was a better way to manage the transition here, with less risk to personnel and aircraft. Perhaps some of the surplus Harvards at Masterton could be transferred to Wigram. Getting the trainee pilots at Wigram into the Harvards for some exposure to a heavier and more complex aeroplane, before allowing them to take on the Kittyhawk in Masterton, would improve things. *Let's see what OC Training at Wigram thinks about it*, he thought as he flew south.

John was not enjoying his flight. He had experienced turbulent conditions as he had departed the station at Masterton. Then, later in his flight, he had encountered some more rough air at altitude, in the strong north-westerly conditions prevailing. Looking ahead as he flew south over the Wairarapa area, John could see there were rolls of cloud streaming off some of the peaks to his west. *Keep away from those*, he reminded himself. He knew they indicated areas where there would be severe turbulence.

Once clear of Wairarapa, and out over the sea, John was soon flying parallel to a mountain range known as the Kaikouras, situated on the northeast coast of New Zealand's South Island. He was about five miles out to sea, and some one hundred and fifty miles north of Christchurch. The turbulence was not as bad as it had been, but he found his aircraft would not climb above 20,000 feet. He realised immediately what was happening. The strong westerly-quarter wind over the Kaikoura Ranges, with some peaks reaching over 8,000 feet, had caused a mountain wave. On the lee side of the mountains, where he was flying, the air mass was descending after crossing the ranges. He was struggling to maintain altitude, even with his power set higher than normal and holding a slight nose-up attitude. *Damn, this is powerful*, John thought, as he watched his rate of descent indicator show that despite his aircraft's power and attitude configuration, he was slowly losing altitude. His airspeed was fluctuating sharply too, as the Kittyhawk experienced occasional bouts of turbulence. A lenticular cloud above the Kaikouras, with its stacked saucer-like appearance, confirmed he was in severe wave conditions. However, he was relieved to be flying through clear air, with no cloud or icing. It would have been much more difficult if he was flying blind, with ice building on his aircraft.

After another twenty minutes he flew clear of the invisible wave of downward moving air, and he could once again maintain his chosen altitude without difficulty.

When John arrived at RNZAF Wigram, he greeted Malcolm Johns, Officer Commanding Training there.

'Those mountain waves along the Kaikouras are powerful. I struggled to maintain twenty thousand,' John commented after he and Malcolm had completed their initial introduction formalities.

'Fairly common along those ranges in strong nor-west conditions,' Malcom responded. 'If you want to get out of it, you fly further away, downwind, from the ranges.'

'I was in a Kittyhawk. Plenty of power and robust. How would it have been for one of your students in a Tiger Moth?'

'No good at all, but we don't send them out on days like that — certainly not near mountainous terrain.'

'I can understand that,' John acknowledged, before moving on to the purpose of their meeting and his proposal to integrate some Harvard instruction into the flying courses at RNZAF Wigram.

By the afternoon, having reached an agreement on developing the flying training at Wigram to a higher level, John was taxiing for take-off. He was pleased with the outcome of his meeting. The Officer Commanding Training at Wigram had thought John's idea a good one. He, too, was keen to develop his training programme using Harvards.

'I might even put an out-of-hours aircraft up as a gate guardian as you enter RNZAF Wigram. A Harvard would look better than the Tiger Moth I was contemplating,' Malcolm had laughed.

John was now to fly to RNZAF Taieri, the Air Force station located at the northern end of a natural basin, just south of Dunedin. He was to meet with the station CO at Taieri to discuss progress on the Elementary Flying School being established there. Then he would stay overnight and return to Masterton the next day.

John was twenty miles north of the small grass aerodrome that constituted RNZAF Taieri. As he approached the basin in which the aerodrome was situated, and with Dunedin city off his port wing, he decided a quick diversion to the Clydevale area would enable him to say hello to his family. It was only thirty-eight miles away according to his map, about eight minutes in the Kittyhawk. He rolled slightly to the right and began tracking along the western side of the Taieri basin. Soon, Greenfield, the area near Clydevale where his family farmed, loomed ahead. John increased power and eased the Kittyhawk down to a lower height as it accelerated through the smooth air. He had decided he would make a high-speed pass over the farm, at a low level. Sitting in the cockpit, with three hundred and fifty-five miles per hour showing on his air speed indicator, he grinned broadly. The Kittyhawk's supercharged Allison V-12 sang. Descending to what he estimated to be two hundred feet above ground level, John made a fast pass over the family homestead, before pulling into a steep climb. The aircraft was going up quickly as John turned and dived back towards the homestead, levelling at about two hundred feet above the ground again as he roared overhead. Then he entered a wide orbit, circling the farm, rocking his wings to wave to anyone watching below. He saw a figure near the barn and thought it was probably his father. *Hope he liked that pass.*

Three hours later, John was back at the farm, this time in a car he had borrowed from one of the officers at Taieri. He was programmed to overnight at Dunedin, so it had been easy enough to arrange to stay with his parents instead. He was not due out of Taieri until noon the next day. He was sitting at the old white oak dining table in the homestead's kitchen, having a "pre-dinner dram" as his father always called it. John was enjoying his whisky, and enjoying being home, even if for only a short time.

'It's wonderful you are here, John,' his mother, Lillian, exclaimed. 'So much has happened in the world since you left, we weren't sure when we might see you again. We did read about you in the paper, getting your medal from King George. What was he like?'

John smiled. His mother was an ardent royalist, and he knew she would be very keen to hear all the details about what had happened at Buckingham Palace when he had received his DFC after the Battle of Britain. He almost felt sorry for the members of her local stitch group. They would have had lots of commentary about it from her at their monthly meetings.

'The king was a very friendly chap,' John said, affectionately squeezing his mother's hand. 'It's good to be back here.'

Sitting in the familiar kitchen where he had grown up, John felt a warm sense of contentment. The Luftwaffe and the Imperial Japanese Army Air Force seemed a long way away. He felt safe here, completely detached from the realities of war.

The following day, and just under two hours since he had taken off from the grass strip at RNZAF Taieri, a few miles south of Dunedin, John was approaching to land back at Hood Aerodrome, RNZAF Masterton.

The return flight had been uneventful, and John had been able to relax and think about the evening he had enjoyed with his parents. It had been wonderful to catch up with them after nearly four years away. He knew it might be some time before he saw them again. His brother Tom, who had taken over John's farm role when he had left to join the RAF, had not been home. John had been sorry to have missed seeing him on his brief visit, but it had been unavoidable.

'He's joined up,' his father had said when John had asked where Tom was. 'He's in Auckland, helping at the flying boat base in Hobsonville. He volunteered as soon as New Zealand joined Great Britain in declaring war on Germany, and was away within the month.'

John was not surprised that New Zealand had been quick to support Britain in the war. Despite being at opposite ends of the world, there had always been a closeness between the two countries, quite apart from the fact that they were both members of the Commonwealth.

After landing back at Hood aerodrome, RNZAF Masterton, John went into the officers' mess.

'Good trip, sir?' Richard asked cheerily. He had been left in charge, and it looked like he had taken good care of everything while John had been away.

'Thanks. All went well with my training meetings. We are sending Harvards down to Wigram, so they can better prepare pilots for the Kittyhawks we will put them into when they arrive here for their advanced training. I also had an interesting experience with mountain waves along the Kaikoura coast. I hadn't struck them before. Fair bit of unwanted natural power there — a pilot could get into trouble if in cloud and wanting to maintain altitude.'

'Mountain waves? Yes, they are testing, and dangerous if you don't react appropriately,' Richard agreed. 'Nevertheless, turning downwind to fly out of the effect is the way to go. That will get you out of the wave, if necessary.'

'I also had time to catch up with my folks while I was in the South,' John said, 'so that was good. I hadn't seen them since leaving New Zealand to join the RAF.'

'I'm sure they're very proud of you, sir,' Richard replied with a smile.

*

Over the next few months, John and Richard worked hard to train the new pilots in their squadron. As John had expected, the preliminary training in the Harvards at RNZAF Wigram now available made pilot transition to the Kittyhawks at Masterton much easier and safer, and he was pleased with how far they had come.

In what seemed like no time at all, it was time for him to leave New Zealand once more. The evening before his departure, Wing Commander Matthews came to give him a proper send-off.

'Squadron Leader Noble, it's my honour to speak on the occasion of your farewell. Over recent months you have established the squadron and led the programme to transform its members into capable fighter pilots in our Kittyhawk aircraft. We all appreciate what you have done, and how important it's going to be for us in the coming months when we meet the forces of Japan up in the Pacific. The aerial warfare experience you have passed on to the pilots will help enormously. Your departure tomorrow is the Royal Air Force's gain, and our loss, but we understand why you have been recalled to Britain. Things will soon be happening there that require people of your calibre and experience. Please know you go with our best wishes and grateful thanks.'

'Hear, hear,' called several of those present.

'To remind you of us all at Masterton, and at Ohakea, please accept this as a token of our appreciation,' Matthews continued, as he passed John a pewter drinking mug. It was engraved with John's name, recording that it was presented to him by *The Commanding Officer, and Officers, RNZAF Ohakea.*

'Thank you,' John responded, before going on to say how much he had enjoyed his time in New Zealand. 'As the CO has noted, I'm going back to England, to again participate in the European theatre. I'm looking forward to being involved there, but first, I have a six-week sea voyage. I'm not too excited about that, but I've no choice. There's no air passage available at present. I appreciate your kind words, and this —' he raised the drinking mug — 'will be put to good use, I assure you. Thank you.'

CHAPTER THIRTEEN

John's voyage to Britain was largely uneventful, apart from a brief scare as the ship was passing the Azores. Early in the morning one day, an alert had been sounded on the vessel's public address system.

'All crew, all crew, report to your emergency station,' it had blared. John, like most others on the boat, was instantly awake. He leapt from his bunk, grabbed his clothes, and started getting dressed as fast as he could. He then ran up the stairs leading to the top deck.

'Get below!' a seaman shouted at him as John emerged through the large doors on that deck. It was no time to argue, so John retreated into the stairwell. There was a porthole there, so he was able to look out over the sea, to the ship's port side. The weather was good, with gentle swells and only the occasional whitecap as some swells crested and broke. *What's caused the alert?* John wondered. *Can't see anything from this side. Maybe something on the other side of the boat?* But nothing happened, and after thirty minutes, John went down to the lounge area on the deck below. Other service personnel were there, some playing cards, some reading. Others were just sitting quietly, mostly watching everyone else's activities.

'What's up? Do you know?' John asked the first person he encountered — an army captain, judging by his uniform.

'Not sure, but one of the seamen said something about a German surface raider being spotted in the area, so maybe it's something to do with that.'

It turned out that they need not have worried. Two hours later, there was a call instructing the crew to stand down. John was relieved the alert had come to nothing. It could have meant the end of his war if there had been an attack.

After his long journey, John finally arrived at RAF Bentley Priory, the headquarters for Fighter Command. He was now meeting Wing Commander Ian Blowers, the officer responsible for managing fighter-pilot postings.

'Squadron Leader Noble, sir, reporting as required following passage from New Zealand.'

'Welcome back to the UK, Squadron Leader,' said Blowers. 'I understand you had some difficult times in Malaya. And since evacuating from Singapore, you have been assisting the RNZAF with advanced training for their fighter pilots?'

'Correct, sir. Bit of an organisational disaster in Singapore. We had inadequate aircraft, both in terms of numbers and capability, and the air-defence warning system was hopeless. Basically, it just didn't operate.'

'I had heard things were not too good there. Questions to be asked of the senior commanders who were there at some time, I suspect. We were all shocked by the speed of the Japanese advance and, not to put too fine a point on it, the speed of the British surrender. Anyway, that's someone else's enquiry for another time. For now, we need to organise your role back here in Britain.'

'I'm very keen to have a fighter squadron again, sir.'

'Sorry, Squadron Leader, there is no current requirement for a new CO in any of our fighter outfits.'

John tried not to show the disappointment he felt, but answered stiffly, 'I have substantial war ops leadership experience. I had hoped that would be needed by one of the squadrons here. As you know, I operated over Dunkirk, in the Battle of Britain, and against the Japanese in Malaya.'

'You don't have to spell it out for me. I'm aware of all that. The fact of the matter is that I have a lot of experienced fighter pilots, any of whom would be ideal as a commanding officer, but all of our squadrons are adequately served at present. I'm sorry.'

'Does Fighter Command have a posting in mind for me, sir?'

'We do. The plan is for you to complete the instructors' course at the Central Gunnery School, RAF Sutton Bridge. Once qualified there — it will take four weeks — you will be posted to Rednal in Shropshire, as OC flight gunnery training.'

That night, John stayed at the visiting officers' quarters at Bentley Priory. *Must ring Mary*, he thought, thinking of his much-missed girlfriend of several years. He had not seen her since leaving for Singapore. They had written regularly but had not spoken. Now he had the chance, he hurried straight to the telephone.

'It's John,' he announced when Mary answered. She was currently living at the nurses' home attached to the hospital where she worked. Normally, Mary lived with her parents, but the increased demands at the hospital had persuaded her it would be more practical if she stayed in the nurses' accommodation. 'I've just arrived back in Britain,' John went on. 'I'm in London tonight, and I've been posted to Sutton Bridge in Lincolnshire. Going there tomorrow.'

'Oh, John, it's so good to hear your voice again. It's been too long. Much too long,' exclaimed Mary.

'And I love hearing you again,' John replied.

'When can we see each other?' Mary asked.

'Not sure about my timetable. I will know more once I get to Sutton Bridge. I'll call you when I have a better idea of what

I'm doing and when we can get together, but it will be soon, I promise.'

'Yes, please,' Mary said.

They talked for nearly twenty minutes before Mary said she had to go.

'Sorry, John, some of the other girls want to use the phone, so I had better finish this call. We'll speak when you know your plans.'

'Bye,' said John softly as she hung up.

Once at Sutton Bridge, John realised the gunnery course was going to be more interesting than he had anticipated. Like many other pilots who had begun flying at the time he had, John had learnt his aerial shooting skills — apart from some very rudimentary instruction during flight training — from his experience in battle. Hearing the chief instructor outline the rationale behind the specific gunnery training now given to fighter pilots confirmed to John the value of such instruction.

'Pilots are joining squadrons well trained and competent in all aspects of flight. They get engaged in squadron formations and procedures, advanced air combat techniques, and aerial warfare strategy, but there's not much actual shooting practice or study. The objective these days is to ensure a fighter pilot is given some formal shooting training. He needs to understand, and develop his core skills around, gun harmonisation, optimum range, line of flight estimation, deflection requirements, attacking from a dive, from a half-roll, and from what we call an awkward position above or below the target aircraft.'

While there was nothing new in what John heard, he realised his capability as a fighter pilot would have been realised much sooner in his career if he had been specifically trained on gunnery, rather than learning on the job. He was keen to get on and qualify as an instructor so he could begin passing on shooting skills to the new pilots emerging from the flying training schools.

'Here's the final programme for you, Squadron Leader,' the chief instructor said to John on his third day at Sutton Bridge. Finalising the detail had been held up for some reason, so while John had started his training, he had been unsure about when he would be able to visit Mary. 'It's busy, as you can see, but we are keen to get you qualified as soon as possible.'

John was disappointed that his training programme meant he would not get anything more than an occasional day off during the entire four-week course. One day off provided insufficient time to travel to see Mary in Yorkshire. But he saw that he would have three days free between finishing his instructor's course and starting at Rednal, so he decided he would use those days to catch up with Mary. It would also mean that she would have plenty of time to arrange her own leave from the hospital. He decided to call her that evening to let her know the arrangements.

'May I speak to Mary Harridge, please?' John asked the nurse who answered the telephone when he called the nurses' home.

'Who is speaking, please?'

'John Noble. I'm a friend of Mary's.'

'Just a minute, please.'

A few minutes later, there was another voice on the telephone. 'This is Matron Hogg. To whom am I speaking?'

'John Noble.'

'You were calling to speak to Nurse Harridge?'

'Yes.'

'May I ask what your relationship with her is?'

'I've been going out with Mary for nearly three years. I was speaking to her a few days ago. We were planning to meet. I've been overseas on active service, and I'm not long back in Britain.'

'I'm sorry, John. Nurse Harridge was badly injured in a bombing attack in Newcastle last evening. I regret to have to tell you that she died this afternoon.'

John was rigid with shock. He had a flash of Mary's face, smiling at him, followed immediately by a vision of her lying on the ground, burnt and bloodied as the result of a bomb's explosion. His head ached. He felt as if he could not breathe freely. *No, it can't be true. Mary's not dead*, he thought desperately.

'Are you sure it was Mary who was killed? Could it have been someone else?' John pleaded.

'I'm sorry. There is no doubt that it was Nurse Harridge. Please accept my deepest sympathy.'

Tears welled in John's eyes. He could not think clearly.

'I'm so sorry to be the person to have to tell you, John,' the matron continued, but he was no longer listening. His initial shock had now been replaced by an intense anger. Staring at the telephone receiver in his hand, he slammed it back into its cradle. He turned and left the room, stumbling along as if in some kind of stupor, his tears flowing freely.

The people at Central Gunnery School were very understanding. 'Take as many days as you need. We will see you again after the funeral,' the school's commanding officer told John next morning, when he had explained why he would be taking leave.

He travelled up to Yorkshire immediately, to attend Mary's funeral, which was taking place in Thirsk. On the day of the ceremony, John could see the pain in the faces of Mary's parents. Her father tried hard to be stoic, but failed, while her mother spent most of the day weeping. She didn't make things any easier for John when she talked about why Mary had been in Newcastle at the time of the bombing raid.

'She wanted to buy a new dress before she saw you, John,' she said, her tone sharp in spite of her despair. 'She wouldn't have been there if you hadn't telephoned, saying you wanted to see her as soon as you could.'

It was an unfair comment, and it hurt John, but there was nothing he could say that would help. Mary's mother was just speaking with a parent's grief as she tried to make sense of her daughter's death.

Four days later, John was back at the Gunnery School. People had not really got to know him in the short time he had been there before Mary's death. If they had, they would have seen a marked change in his character. Normally friendly and outgoing, John was now largely silent and self-contained, focused on nothing but learning his new skills as an air gunnery instructor. He wanted to be the very best instructor, so his pupils could successfully kill the enemy. Ensuring as many Germans as possible paid the price for Mary's death was now John's principal objective in life, and it drove him on.

When John qualified four weeks later, he was transferred to RAF Rednal as planned. His official title there was Officer Commanding Bombing and Gunnery.

'Welcome to Rednal, Squadron Leader,' the young flight lieutenant who was the station's adjutant said. 'The CO is keen to see you. I will take you along to him now.'

They made their way along a narrow and dimly lit corridor, with broken linoleum showing on parts of the floor.

'Excuse the decor,' the adjutant said with a laugh. 'There's a war on, so nice flooring's not a priority.'

After tapping on the door of the room at the end of the corridor, the adjutant went in. Rednal's Commanding Officer, who had been sitting facing away from the door, swung around to greet his visitors. John was stunned.

'Sir,' the adjutant began, 'may I introduce —'

'No need, Adjutant. I know Squadron Leader Noble well,' said Wing Commander Christopher Bland. 'I was the Squadron Leader's CO at Four-one-five. We flew together over Dunkirk and in the Battle of Britain. Wonderful to see you again.' He smiled at John.

'Hello, sir. I didn't know you were the CO here. This is a surprise.'

'You can leave us now,' Bland said to the adjutant.

Over the next thirty minutes, John and Bland discussed what they had been doing since John had been sent to Singapore. John didn't mention Mary. He was trying to move on, and it hurt to talk about her.

'I'm here because I lost my medical, and I don't think it likely I will ever get it back,' Bland explained. 'It's a good cause here. The young chaps coming through arrive as inexpert aerial shooters, but leave as reasonable quality marksmen. Not much use being a top pilot if you can't shoot your enemy down.'

'Yes, I do appreciate that accurate shooting has not had the attention it deserves during pilot training. I'm keen to pass on my knowledge to the pilots coming through here.'

'The big day is coming soon, when we'll send our forces back across the Channel into France, so we are busy here trying to push the training flights through. I didn't expect my next instructor to be an experienced warhorse like you, but I'm happy to have you, Squadron Leader.'

'Thank you, sir. For my part I'm pleased to be assisting in what is clearly an important training element, although to be honest, I did want an operational squadron. No slot available at present, I was told.'

'I understand your thinking. Valuable as the training here is, if I still had my medical I wouldn't have come to Rednal for this role, but we are obliged to handle the cards we are dealt.'

After John had left Bland's office, he began thinking about his past association with Bland. They had disagreed on many things, and John had been critical of Bland's performance as the leader of 415 Squadron. Thankfully, before John had left for Singapore, there had been something of a rapprochement, and they had been beginning to get on well together. John knew why. A frightening incident in the air had caused Bland to change how he had been behaving, and that had made things better for everyone in 415 Squadron.

Over the following months, John worked hard. While he enjoyed passing on his knowledge and experience, he still hankered for an operational role.

Then, in early September, formal written advice about a new posting arrived in his office. He opened it and read the message, with some surprise:

Squadron Leader John Noble, DFC, is transferred to 645 Squadron, RAF Coltishall, as Commanding Officer, effective 15 September 1943.

John could not believe it. It seemed he was off to Norfolk, back in an operational squadron as its commanding officer, and he knew 645 Squadron operated Spitfires.

He went to find the adjutant. 'Adjutant, I have just received notice of posting to Six-four-five in Coltishall. Is that correct?'

'Six-four-five is correct, sir. Between you and me, I think the CO had something to do with it.'

'Could I see the CO, please?' John wanted to thank Bland for what he had done.

'No, sir. He's on leave for five days. A family matter, I understand.'

'Ah, I will miss him in that case. I leave before he gets back. Could you tell him that I was very pleased to get the posting?'

'Certainly, sir. I will convey your pleasure,' the adjutant replied, with a knowing smile.

The station commander, Group Captain Peter James, called into John's office just a few hours after John's arrival at RAF Coltishall. John was busy sorting his various files and notes and setting his room up as he wanted it.

'Settling in, Squadron Leader Noble?' the group captain asked.

'I am, thank you, sir. I have been away from war ops in this theatre for some time, first in Singapore, and latterly helping the RNZAF with some training in New Zealand, before coming back here. I have been involved with gunnery training over recent months. Things appear to be quite different now. I understand the Luftwaffe isn't currently coming over Britain with anywhere near the frequency or numbers previously experienced.'

'Yes, we aren't seeing the activity there was. In fact, the tables have been turned somewhat. There are now multiple missions by the RAF every day over France, Belgium, and the Netherlands, and the heavy bombers are going right into Germany. We do get the occasional small group of Luftwaffe aircraft trying to penetrate our defences, and some daylight bombing raids still occur from time to time, but principally they're against targets north of Eleven Group's area, where Jerry thinks we have fewer fighters.'

'What's Fighter Command's current focus?' John asked.

'Most of us here have been flying Jim Crows, patrolling off the Dutch coast looking for enemy surface activity, or escorting some of the light bomber missions into France or Belgium, principally.'

'Jim Crows?' John asked. It was not a term he was familiar with.

'Just slang for the coastal patrols we have established to intercept any enemy aircraft coming in over Britain's coastline.'

'Oh, right. Got it,' John responded.

'Join me at my table in the mess tonight. In fact, come in half an hour before dinner, at six, and I'll introduce you to some of the key people in your squadron and on the station.'

When John entered the officers' mess that evening, Peter was already there, and he had assembled a small group to meet John.

'Gentlemen,' Peter said, 'may I introduce Squadron Leader John Noble, the new CO of Six-four-five squadron.'

One by one, the officers introduced themselves to John, who was trying to remember their names and roles. He noted his flight commanders were Flight Lieutenants Roger Edmonds and Alistair Giles. Both men were experienced Spitfire pilots, having flown through the Battle of Britain. Flying Officer Murray Brent was also introduced. He was the squadron's aerial warfare instructor, ensuring the pilots were always up to date with the latest strategies and tactics being employed against German forces, both in the air and on the ground.

'And this is Squadron Leader Wojtek Kowalski, our marvellous aeronautical engineer,' Peter continued, as he introduced John to a dark-haired man of about thirty. 'Wojtek is from Poland, if you hadn't already picked that up from his name. He was studying aeronautics on exchange from Warsaw University at the Martlesham Aeroplane and Armament Experimental Establishment when war broke out. When that operation was moved to Boscombe Down at the outbreak of war, Wojtek was offered a short service commission with the Royal Air Force. He accepted, and here he is — our aeronautical engineering officer, and a very good one at that.'

Over the following weeks, John and Wojtek became firm friends. John had soon learned that, apart from his apparently excellent engineering skills, Wojtek was a very pleasant chap. They talked a lot about their respective pasts, Wojtek showing great interest in New Zealand, and how John's flying career had progressed from the time he had been a farmer. For his part, John was fascinated by the stories Wojtek had to tell of his student days in Warsaw, and some of the things he had been doing at the Experimental Establishment.

John soon settled into his role as Commanding Officer at 645 Squadron. To avoid ad hoc operations, he established a roster system, principally involving Jim Crows and patrols aimed at shipping interdiction off the Dutch coast. Knowing the squadron was going to be called on from time to time to provide a fighter escort to bombing missions being undertaken by American Bostons and RAF Beaufighters, he also ensured he always had aircraft available for any such short-notice missions. Occasionally, the squadron was also asked to join in providing fighter cover to larger bombers, but only for attacks on targets in the western areas of the Continent. The operational range of the squadron's Mk V Spitfires ruled out participation in any longer missions.

Thinking about what was now required from a fighter squadron, compared to what he had known prior to going to

Singapore, John could see the change in fortunes. His squadron's operational agenda reflected the new situation of the German forces. Now it was Britain's aircraft ranging across the Channel to attack them, the reverse of what had been occurring previously. John recognised the progress since the earlier dark days of Britain's air war, and he knew that soon it would be the turn of the ground forces as they went back into Europe.

CHAPTER FOURTEEN

The flight of four Spitfires from 645 Squadron, led by John, had been airborne for thirty-five minutes when trouble occurred. They were some way off England's east coast at the time, partway through their latest Jim Crow. The patrol had begun from RAF Coltishall and progressed north to their current position — approximately fifty miles out to sea from Hartlepool.

The operational briefing for the patrol had been standard.

'Climb to eighteen thousand feet, airborne,' John had told his flight. 'We will operate as a four-ship fleet, in two pairs, the second pair following the first at two hundred yards. Each of a pair's members is to maintain a fifty-yard lateral separation from the other member of that pair. Scan generally, but give the eastern sector additional focus. Any Hun having a go will be coming in from that direction.'

But now the patrol had been interrupted by an urgent call from Alistair Giles, leading the second pair.

'Red One, this is Yellow One. I have an engine problem. Breaking away towards the coast.'

John, Red One on this patrol, glanced back over his left shoulder. He could see Yellow One had turned west and was clearly not able to maintain altitude. Alistair was already a few hundred feet below the patrol's level, and descending.

'Yellow One, I see you. What's your engine status?'

'I've reduced power due to a strong vibration. Showing loss of oil pressure, and the temperature's increasing. It's not going to last. Ah, engine's gone. No power at all now. Establishing best glide speed.'

John quickly made some calculations in his head as he watched Alistair's aircraft descending towards the distant English coastline. *Damn, he can't glide as far as the coast, especially with the westerly we have today*, he thought in dismay.

'I think you may be beyond gliding distance from land, Yellow One. Intentions?' he called.

'Yes, that's my view too. I don't want to try a water landing. These machines aren't great to ditch at the best of times, and I see what looks like a sizeable swell down there, anyway. I'll bale out once down to three thousand. At least that will have me in the water, closer to the coast. My quick estimate has me coming down about ten to twelve miles out.'

'I will stick with you until you are ready to exit, then circle as long as I can while Coastal Command gets organised to pick you up. You have your dinghy?'

'Certainly do. I don't take on extended over-water trips without checking it's there, and undamaged. I can't swim.'

John smiled. 'Yellow Two, take my place and continue the patrol with Red Two, as a pair. I'm going to stay with Yellow One.'

With the standard call of "*wilco*" from Yellow Two, the two Spitfires designated to continue the patrol reformed and continued tracking north towards their turn position abeam Newcastle.

John positioned himself alongside Alistair, who was now descending through sixteen thousand feet.

'I have done all the checks, and I have been unable to restart. Mind you, it has failed because of some sort of oil problem, so no surprise I can't get it going again.'

'Roger. Just keep heading towards shore, maintaining best glide speed,' John replied.

Ten minutes later, as they were passing through six thousand feet, John asked, 'Are you okay?'

'Yes, just checking my exit and parachute drills. To be honest, I'm a bit nervous, but I prefer to jump than ditch. Sea's too rough for ditching. Hitting a wave at touchdown would be like running into a brick wall.'

'Coastal Command is putting something up as soon as they can, in response to my call to them about your planned bale-out, but I expect you will have to float around a bit before they turn up.'

'Hope they've got sharp eyes,' Alistair responded.

A short while later, he called John again. 'Passing three thousand, setting up to exit.'

At that transmission from Alistair, John looked towards his Spitfire, one hundred yards out to his left. Alistair had slid his cockpit canopy back and pitched the nose of his aircraft up slightly, to slow it down. Then, as John watched, he saw the aircraft slowly roll inverted. Alistair came out of his cockpit and fell clear. Moments later, his parachute blossomed and he floated down, relatively gently, towards the sea, now about two thousand feet below.

Once in the sea, it did not take Alistair long to inflate his emergency life raft and get himself into it. He waved as John made a low pass at two hundred feet, rocking his wings to show he had seen he was safe. *Hope the boys in the Catalina aren't too far away*, John thought as he reported Alistair's successful parachute exit, noting the pilot was now in his life raft, approximately eleven miles east of Hartlepool.

After fifty minutes, John's fuel state meant he had to divert to an aerodrome to refuel. He could not continue circling. *Where's that Catalina?* he wondered. He flew low over Alistair, rocking his wings again, and then set off for RAF Catterick. He knew there was no longer any fuel available at the old Hartlepool training facility, the closest aerodrome. Catterick was only an additional ten minutes' flying time from Hartlepool, so it was no problem to go there.

As John was waiting for his aircraft to be refuelled, he found himself thinking about the day's events. He decided he would chat to Wojtek when he got back to Coltishall. He wanted to be sure they did not have a reliability trend emerging. There had been another report recently about one of the Spitfires having a low oil pressure alert.

With refuelling complete, John was soon airborne again, climbing east out of Catterick. Once back in the area where Alistair had come down, John began a sweep, scanning the sea surface as he flew, trying to relocate Alistair. He saw the search and rescue Catalina had now arrived in the area, and it was similarly searching for the downed Spitfire pilot. They reported no contact when John checked with them on his radio.

After thirty minutes of searching, with no sign of Alistair, John felt his concern growing. More than two hours in the open sea in a small life raft was too long, especially when it was a rough and choppy North Sea. Twenty minutes later, John was still flying a standard search pattern, back and forth, looking for any sign of a dinghy. Estimating distance from the coastline was not a precise exercise, but it was sufficient to enable an effective grid search, and the Catalina was looking too. *We should have found him by now*, John thought. *It will be dark in fifteen minutes, then we won't have any chance of seeing him.*

Just then, the Catalina radioed to say that it would be abandoning the search soon. An RAF search and rescue launch had been sent out from Teesmouth to help and should be in the search area within ten minutes, the Catalina crew confirmed. John knew that airborne searching could not continue in the dark, so he understood the launch being sent to continue once the aircraft left the area. He looked at his watch as he turned to fly yet another line in the pattern he had established to look for Alistair. A few minutes later, he saw the launch. White water broke around its bow as it pushed through the choppy sea. *At least we have a means to pick Alistair up if we can find him*, he thought, but he was feeling grim. *Okay, one last sweep, then I will have to vacate too.*

Another sweep. Nothing. John was feeling down. No commanding officer wants to lose one of his squadron members, particularly when it is the result of something as avoidable as an aircraft malfunction. It just did not seem fair. He turned his Spitfire to track home towards RAF Coltishall, crossing in front of the searching launch as he did so. Just then, a red flare arced up from the sea, about half a mile to the south. The boat crew saw it too. The launch altered course towards the area from where the flare had been fired. John circled to watch. Two large searchlights on the foredeck of the launch lit up the ocean surface.

There he is, John thought, elated that Alistair had been found. He could see the small life raft, with a figure now sitting up in it and waving frantically in the beam of the lights.

'Thought I was a goner,' Alistair said. It was midday on the day following his rescue, and he had just arrived by car back at Coltishall. He was in John's office, speaking with John, and Roger Edmonds.

'Yes, but you were found and that's what matters,' John replied with a grin. 'One question: I had been running a grid search in the area for some time before the launch arrived, so why didn't you fire your flare earlier?'

'Couldn't get it to work. I was bloody angry, sir. I've always carried a Very pistol with me in case I come down somewhere inhospitable. I heard you in the vicinity, but could I get the thing to fire? No.'

'So what changed?'

There was silence for a moment. John sensed that Alistair was slightly embarrassed. He waited.

'Didn't release the safety properly.'

For a moment John said nothing. Then he and Roger both started laughing. Alistair, known as a particularly careful and well-prepared operator, had made a simple mistake that was nearly very costly. Then Alistair joined in, laughing at himself. John recognised it was more about releasing tension than expressing humour — an acknowledgement of a happy ending to what could have been a disaster.

The next morning, John went to see Wojtek Kowalski. He found him in the maintenance hangar, looking flustered and appearing to be under considerable pressure.

'You being pushed, Woj?' John asked, using the nickname he had adopted whenever he spoke to Wojtek.

'Only because the parts I ask for never arrive when they say they will, or sometimes they send me the wrong things. It drives me angry,' the Pole replied, using his own idiom.

'Well, I hope I'm not going to make it worse for you, but we have had two oil pressure problems recently, one of them resulting in the loss of an aircraft after the engine failed.'

'Ach, I know, I know. I have a theory, but I can't tell you about it now. Too busy this morning. What about over lunch at the café outside the gates? Mrs Meade's Tearooms — it's my favourite place. I spend a lot of time there.'

'Done. See you there at one o'clock — that suit?'

'Okay, and I will pay. My treat,' Wojtek replied with a smile.

Three hours later, Wojtek and John were sitting at a small table on the veranda of Mrs Meade's Tearooms. John was not that hungry, so just had scones and tea. Somehow, despite the restrictions caused by the war, Mrs Meade had managed to get some strawberry jam and cream to go with the scones. Wojtek ordered a sausage of some kind. It was small but, he confirmed, very tasty. John was surprised a meal involving meat was available.

'Mrs Meade must think you're special, Woj. How the hell do you get a sausage, with all the restrictions? Thought I had done well with cream and jam, but a sausage — well, I need to come here more often.'

'She thinks I'm special. She looks after me, and any friend I bring along,' Wojtek said with a short laugh. 'I've been thinking about your query regarding oil pressure, John. First thing to ensure is that there is sufficient oil at start-up. I will instruct the fitters to check dipsticks first thing each morning, before operations begin. It's normally done last thing at night, but that wouldn't pick up any leakage occurring between then and morning. I doubt it's a likely cause of the problem, but let's rule it out by doing that.'

John nodded his agreement as Wojtek continued.

'I've already checked viscosity. It's okay, so that's not the problem. Then we get into the more complex stuff — clogged filters, relief valve seating failure, or pump issues. The plan is to check four aircraft per night for these issues. That's all we have time for overnight, but we will be through them all in four nights.'

'Thanks, Woj, that's very helpful. Let me know if you find anything as you proceed. And thank you for lunch. The scones and jam were magnificent.'

'Ha — spoken like a man starved of treats by wartime rationing.'

John knew that was true. Then he thought about his mother's expertise in producing scones back on the farm in New Zealand and felt a momentary pang of homesickness.

'When do you think our troops will go over, John?' Wojtek asked.

'No-one knows, apart from those planning it, but soon, I suspect.'

'I so look forward to the end of this war. I want to go back to Poland and see my family.'

'Are they having any difficulties with the Nazis?' John asked.

'There have been bad things happening in Warsaw, but they are all right. They seem to have avoided the worst of what the Germans have done, but it has been terrible for some of those caught up in it.'

'Good to hear your family is fine, Wojtek. Difficulties for them would be horrible for you.'

'Yes, they would. Let's talk about something else. John, did you know one of the other squadrons at the station is putting on a concert tomorrow night, in the number two maintenance hangar? They needed my agreement for that, which I gave them, on the condition that they let me have the two best seats at the front. You want to be my guest?'

'Thanks, Woj. I would like that,' John said with a grin. He liked Wojtek, and Wojtek clearly enjoyed John's friendship.

Apart from patrols off the east coast of England, looking for any German aircraft trying to mount a raid, the squadron spent a lot of its time over the following weeks operating out towards the Dutch coast.

'As well as patrolling our coast, to interdict any inbound enemy elements, squadrons should operate regular patrols off the Netherlands, strafing any shipping encountered,' had been the instruction from Fighter Command.

John understood the strategy was to interfere with the movement of equipment and troops along the enemy-occupied coastline. That disruption would be useful in the period leading up to the much-anticipated Allied invasion. When and where the invasion would occur were not known by anyone other than those in the highest military positions, but it would happen soon, most thought. The Pas de Calais, adjacent to the shortest stretch of water between England and France, was thought most likely to be the landing area.

John first heard about his squadron's role in the proposed Allied invasion of Europe at a meeting of Eleven and Twelve Group Commanding Officers held at RAF Uxbridge in late April. After a general briefing, which confirmed what everyone knew anyway — that the Allies would soon cross the Channel to confront the occupying German forces — the role of RAF Fighter Command in the invasion was discussed. For 645 Squadron, there was to be an immediate relocation south, to an aerodrome near Brighton.

When back at Coltishall, John called a briefing and addressed his squadron, bringing them up to date with Fighter Command's plans to support the invasion.

'We are to move to an airfield at Deanland, not far from Brighton. It's officially known as Number One-four-nine Airfield,' he said. 'Date and place have not yet been confirmed, but when the invasion does occur, we have been designated to provide a series of patrols over specific landing areas. We will be intercepting enemy aircraft, maybe bombers, maybe fighters, probably both, whenever they try to mount attacks against our ground forces. I am satisfied we are well prepared and ready. Our aircraft are in top shape, thanks to our maintenance people, led by Squadron Leader Kowalski. And our pilots will be a force to be reckoned with in the air, thanks to the specialist training we have undertaken, led by Flying Officer Brent.'

As he spoke, John was feeling relieved that the oil pressure issues had not recurred. Wojtek had ensured the squadron's Spitfires were checked, as promised, and apart from one aircraft with a defective oil ring, no issues had been found that could cause loss of oil pressure.

After the meeting, Wojtek fell into step with John as he made his way back to the administration block.

'So, we're off to the south to prepare for the invasion,' he said. 'I've spent time in Brighton, so I know the area. Didn't know there was a station there. Airfields are usually named after a local town or area, but this is Aerodrome One-four-nine. Very cloak-and-dagger, John. I suppose numbers help keep a location more discreet.'

'Think you're probably right about that, Woj,' John agreed.

'I hadn't expected we would be sent south. It's a bit more distance to get to Pas de Calais. Do you think that might indicate they are planning some other landing area on the French coast, John?'

'I don't know the answer to that, but it certainly isn't as close to Pas de Calais as might have been expected for fighters providing air cover to landing forces there. Maybe all the fields closer are up to capacity with other aircraft.'

'Other aircraft? What types are you talking about?'

'I have heard mention of gliders being used, and paratroopers, so maybe the aircraft supporting those operations?' John said, with a shrug. 'What all this does indicate is that it's getting close. We are to be established at Airfield One-four-nine, and ready to operate, within four days.'

'Then the Germans will cop it, and I will be very happy. My family may be safe soon,' Wojtek responded, smiling broadly.

The next twenty-four hours were extremely busy for the squadron as they prepared to transfer to their invasion base, but late in the evening, the station's commanding officer, Group Captain Peter James, called John into his office. As John entered, he could see there was a visitor. A civilian was sitting opposite the group captain's desk. He was unsmiling and looked distant.

'Squadron Leader, I am sorry about the short notice for this meeting, but an important matter has come up. I won't hold you up any longer than necessary. I appreciate you are busy with arrangements to relocate your squadron, but would you answer any questions this gentleman has for you?'

The thin-faced man began speaking. 'My name doesn't matter, but I am from MI5. We are investigating what we think may be espionage being undertaken by someone in the village here.'

John said nothing, but he was wondering what this had to do with him.

'We have information indicating a person of interest, whom we have identified, is regularly meeting with an officer from this station — from your squadron, in fact.'

Someone from the squadron working with a German agent? thought John. *I doubt it.*

'Who is the officer?' he asked.

'Squadron Leader Kowalski.'

John was stunned. 'I doubt Squadron Leader Kowalski would work with any German agent. He is a dedicated officer doing a very good job of keeping our Spitfires airworthy, and he hates the Germans, especially for what they have done to Poland.'

'Maybe, but he does spend a lot of time with the person we think is a spy, the owner of a café next to the station.'

'Mrs Meade, of Mrs Meade's Tearooms?' John asked. 'He goes there a lot, but that's because he likes the food on offer, not to see a spy.'

'Mrs Meade is not who she claims to be. She was formerly a student at Cambridge,' the gaunt man from MI5 responded. 'After completing her undergraduate degree in science in nineteen thirty-eight, she went on to do a masters in applied mathematics, but she discontinued when war broke out. On her initial entry into Britain for her studies, she registered as having come from France, Marseille to be precise, but we have discovered that information is false. Her real name is Gerda Meaden, and she is not from Marseille. She is from Hamburg. She lied to immigration authorities about her background when she came here early in nineteen thirty-six. Why would she do that? Well, we think the Nazis were positioning capable agents in Britain some years prior to the war, anticipating what may happen, and she was one of them.'

'Suspicion about the identity and background of Mrs Meade is one thing, but suggesting Squadron Leader Kowalski may be passing information to her is another. As I said, he is a dedicated and capable officer and has no time for the Germans. He has often expressed his concerns for his family in Warsaw because of the occupation there.'

'I understand your loyalty to a fellow squadron officer, but consider these things, Squadron Leader Noble. A woman claiming to be Glenda Meade from France is in fact Gerda Meaden from Germany, so there has been deceit. We have detected coded radio transmissions, and triangulation has identified a source at or very near the tearooms she runs. On every occasion we detected a transmission, Gerda Meaden has been home at the time. We broke the code and the content is telling; in recent days it has included the name of the aerodrome to which you are moving tomorrow, and a suggestion that, as a consequence, the Pas de Calais may not be the invasion force's landing area. Gerda Meaden looks to be associated with covert radio transmissions containing valuable military information. That information relates to your squadron, and one of your officers has been observed visiting her premises on numerous occasions. You understand now why we are here talking to you, and why we think we have identified her source?'

John had to admit that there was a case to be investigated, so far as Gerda Meaden was concerned, but he felt Wojtek's involvement was just based on circumstantial evidence. 'What are you looking for from me, or is this just advisory?' he asked, feeling despondent.

'We want to set a trap. You are to tell Squadron Leader Kowalski there is a change of plan, and you have been asked to move the squadron to Hornchurch, not down to Deanland. If that information is then heard in a transmission, we will know.'

John felt even more despondent now. *If they are right, and Wojtek is involved, that will be devasting,* he thought.

'I can do that, and it will obviously have to be done tonight to be effective, given our impending relocation.'

'Thank you, Squadron Leader. Get it underway now, please.'

CHAPTER FIFTEEN

John found Wojtek in his office at the back of the main maintenance hangar.

'Excuse me, Woj, got a moment?'

'Sure. What is it this time? There haven't been any more oil pressure issues, I hope.'

'No. All good there, thanks. I wondered if you felt like taking ten for a cocoa.'

'Oh, that's nice of you, rescuing a poor chap from his evening workload, making sure all is good for the squadron's transit. Yes, I can do that. A ten-minute break would be good. Let's go.'

Settled in some comfortable leather armchairs in the officers' mess, John and Wojtek chatted amiably over the cups of cocoa they had made themselves in the kitchen. John was racked with guilt over what he had been asked to do, but he accepted it was necessary. *I just hope they are wrong,* he thought.

Thinking about the task the man from MI5 had given him, John had decided he would be subtle in how he went about what he had to do. His first thought had been to ensure he did not set the trap too early. That might make things too obvious.

'Heard from Warsaw lately, Woj? Hopefully things remain okay with all yours over there.'

John thought he saw a brief flash of unhappiness in Wojtek's eyes, as he replied, 'They are fine, thanks, John.' Then Wojtek changed the subject and began talking about his maintenance team and how pleased he was with their skill and commitment. 'Good at what they do, and nothing's ever a problem, at any time,' he said. 'They're a great team, just what we need with what's coming. In that regard, no suggestion of a date and place yet?'

Armed with the knowledge he now had following his meeting with the MI5 officer, John saw the question as suspicious. He began thinking about previous conversations he had had with Wojtek. He now recalled that questions about the invasion had often been included in their chats. This was his opportunity to do what must be done.

'No, but our orders have been changed. We are now to reposition the squadron to Hornchurch, not south to Aerodrome One-four-nine, at Deanland.'

'Oh,' said Wojtek, leaning forward and whispering, 'do you think that means it is Pas de Calais after all?'

'No idea, Woj, but that's what we have to do, and there will be a reason for it. We've been told to be at peak operational readiness by end of the first week of May, so wherever the landings take place, it looks like they will be soon.'

That was all John said about those matters, and Woj did not ask any more questions, instead chatting amiably about various things going on around the station. After a few minutes, the cocoa was finished and their meeting was over. Woj said he had to get back to oversee some maintenance work the fitters were doing to one of the Spitfires.

John was left feeling depressed over having set a trap for one of his friends. *Hope nothing comes of it*, he thought.

First thing the next day, John was back in the station commander's office. The man from MI5 was there.

'Developments overnight,' Peter said grimly.

The Secret Service officer began speaking, in what John interpreted to be a sombre tone. 'At two this morning, a brief radio transmission was picked up. It emanated from the same area in the village as previously. This is a decode of the intercepted message.' He handed a sheet of paper to John.

It read: *W2 M. PC ref. Aero H not D*

'What does it mean?' John asked.

'Well, I can tell you that what you are looking at is not in the form of the message transmitted. Our codebreakers have produced what you see, and our view is that it is shorthand for: *Second week of May. Pas de Calais noted. Aircraft to Hornchurch not Deanland.*'

John's eyes were fixed on the paper. He could not believe it. 'What happens now?' he asked as he passed back the transcript. It was a brief message, but sufficient to show Wojtek's guilt.

'Squadron Leader Kowalski will be arrested, charged with spying, and held in custody pending trial,' the officer from MI5 said. 'Gerda Meaden will also be arrested, but not immediately. To take her now would indicate we know about her. Then, anything she has submitted recently would be treated with suspicion. German intelligence would probably consider there was a risk we had fed a known agent false information. Because the squadron is moving to another base, she will not know that Kowalski has been arrested, well certainly not for some days. Nothing is to be said to anyone outside this room about this. Confirmed, gentlemen? Official Secrets Act and all that. It automatically applies to you as commissioned officers, and this is certainly designated an official secret.'

Peter and John mumbled their acknowledgement.

'When will the arrest occur?' John asked.

'Military Police will be here at eleven hundred hours to pick up Squadron Leader Kowalski.'

John left the meeting soon after and began walking towards the mess. On the way, he met Wojtek.

'Good morning, John,' he called.

John did not reply immediately, wishing he had not run into his friend.

'Everything okay?' Wojtek asked. 'You seem preoccupied.'

'Sure, everything's fine,' John replied. He struggled to maintain a normal facade as he talked, and decided to end the conversation. 'I'm just off for a brief walk around the station, Woj.'

'Good idea. I'll come with you.'

There was nothing John could do but agree. To say he wanted to be alone would have looked strange.

As they walked, Wojtek talked about his love of aeronautical engineering, and how lucky he was to be in England rather than back home in Warsaw. John talked about his own family back in New Zealand, on their South Otago farm.

'My family is lucky, Woj,' John said. 'Geography means they don't suffer enemy action in the way many in Europe and here in Britain have suffered. To them, the war is a distant event they read about in the newspapers and hear about on the radio.'

'Do you think the Japanese forces might change that?' Wojtek asked.

'I don't think so. Their attack on Pearl Harbor brought the Americans into the war, and the Japanese are likely to be pushed back now.'

'Your country has become involved by sending soldiers and airmen to Britain and North Africa. It has also been involved in Asia, as you well know after your Singapore experience. And your navy has been involved as well, so while you haven't been attacked at home, you've been caught up as part of the Allied effort, and that's all appreciated by the British, from what I see.'

'Thanks, Woj. I'm just sorry your family is caught in the middle of it in Poland.'

To John's surprise, Wojtek burst into tears and sobbed aloud.

'I'm sorry, John. Please excuse me. I have been carrying an awful burden.'

'What is it, Woj?' John was shocked by the depth of emotion Wojtek was showing. 'What's wrong?'

'I told you my family was relatively safe in their home in Warsaw. That is not true. My parents, and my younger sister, are being held by the Nazis.'

'Why would they do that? They are civilians, and they aren't Jewish, so why focus on them?'

'Because I am here,' Wojtek replied. 'They ask me for information about things like how many aircraft there are on the station and what I know of any invasion plans, and I must tell them if we are instructed to move to another base.'

'Do you give it to them?' John asked.

'If I don't, they will kill my family. They say they will start with my sister, but only after she has been tortured in front of my parents. Then they will kill my mother, then my father, and their deaths will not be quick, they promise. I had no choice, John.'

Oh Christ, thought John. *You poor chap.* He put his arm around Wojtek's shoulder. 'I understand, Woj. I don't know how I would have reacted if it had happened to me, but I might have succumbed to their demands too, to protect my family. How do they communicate with you?'

'I chat with Mrs Meade when I go to her café. She is the person I must talk to, and she tells me how my family is doing, and reminds me of the consequences for them if I do not provide information, or if I tell the authorities here what is happening. I've been close to refusing to cooperate, but I can't kill my family.'

'Let's get back, Woj,' John suggested. He knew Wojtek only had a few hours of freedom left, and he wanted to speak to Peter and, if possible, the MI5 officer, before any arrest occurred. There were things they needed to know.

'Excuse me, sir, we need to have a chat about Squadron Leader Kowalski,' John said, shutting Peter's office door behind him as he came in. This was to be a private conversation.

'What is it?'

'I've just been speaking to him. He decided to tell me he had been passing information to a German agent, whom he confirmed as Meade. He said he had been forced to do it to prevent his parents and sister being executed by the Germans. They are being held in Warsaw.'

'What prompted him to tell you? Have you said anything?'

'No, I've said nothing. I'm conscious of my obligations,' John replied, bristling. 'He just decided to unload on me. He's in a dreadful position.'

'All right, but we need to advise MI5 he has made an admission. I have the number of the officer we have been dealing with. His name is Scandrett. He has gone back to where he's staying in the village, planning to return when the MPs are due here for the arrest, at eleven hundred hours. I'll call him now.'

Thirty minutes later, Colonel John Scandrett came in.

'Please tell me exactly what Kowalski said to you, Squadron Leader,' he said.

John took him through the conversation, detailing all he could remember. The colonel sat in silence, making notes, as John spoke.

When he finished, Colonel Scandrett said, 'I want to take Kowalski into custody immediately. He has admitted he is a spy, and I think there's a risk he may decide to disappear.'

'We know now why he did what he did. Does that change anything?' John asked.

'If you spy, you spy. It doesn't matter why you do it.'

'Something to be taken into account, surely?' John queried, desperately. 'Mitigation at sentencing, perhaps?'

'You need to understand there are no shades of grey when it comes to spying, Squadron Leader. There is nothing that can mitigate treason. Death by hanging is mandatory for the offence. Of course, there is also the possibility he will be shot trying to escape before his trial.'

'I doubt he will attempt to get away,' John replied. 'He's much more likely to rely on a judge being more lenient, taking into account the threats made against his family by the Germans. That's what made him act in the way he did.'

'You misunderstand, Squadron Leader. He is clearly guilty of spying. He has admitted it. The death sentence is mandatory. His Majesty's government has no interest in any rationale for why he might have done it. Justice will only be served by his execution. People are dying every day in this war, and Kowalski may have contributed to that in some way. A trial takes time, effort, and money. If that can be avoided, it will be, provided he still pays the ultimate price. That is why he may be shot before his trial, as he tries to escape. Understand?'

John understood. Wojtek would be arrested, charged, and interrogated regarding his activities. When the authorities had all they needed, he would be executed. The thought of this filled John with misery.

There was a knock on the door, and an airman entered. 'Sir, there are some military policemen here looking for a Colonel Scandrett.'

The colonel stood up. 'That's me,' he said. 'Let's go and get the bugger.'

They found Wojtek in his office at the rear of the engineering hangar. Initially, there was no response to the sharp rap on the door. One of the policemen tried to turn the handle. It was locked. Colonel Scandrett was just signalling the policemen to force the door, when it opened, and Wojtek stood there, peering at them.

'Yes?' he asked, and then, as he took in the scene, he looked at John with shock. 'Oh no, you have told them.'

The two military policemen stepped forward and each gripped one of Wojtek's arms.

'Squadron Leader Wojtek Kowalski, you are hereby arrested on suspicion of espionage in a time of war. You will accompany us to a secure place, where you will be formally charged,' Colonel Scandrett recited.

Wojtek did not struggle, nor did he say anything. He simply stared at John the whole time, even as he was led away. It was as if he could not believe his friend had so quickly called the authorities.

Later that morning, John called a hasty meeting and addressed his squadron.

'Our relocation to Deanland has been delayed,' he said. 'The delay is the result of an event you are no doubt aware of by now. Squadron Leader Kowalski has been arrested and charged with espionage.' John still insisted on referring to Wojtek by his proper rank. 'The Security Services want to talk to those of you who were working with the squadron leader, or who saw him socially. It's nothing for you to worry about — they just need to ensure that any relevant information is passed to the authorities as soon as possible. If you are in one of those categories, please come to my office after this so we may get your details and schedule a time for you to meet with investigators. I would be grateful if you would all treat this matter as highly confidential. We don't want any third party Squadron Leader Kowalski has dealt with becoming aware of his arrest at this time. Thank you.'

The interviews by the Security Service did not take long. No-one who had worked with Wojtek had noticed anything unusual, and it turned out that apart from John, Wojtek had not socialised much with other squadron officers.

MI5 had picked over every word John and Wojtek had ever uttered together, so far as John could remember, particularly what was said when Wojtek had decided to tell John about his family and what he had done. John had noticed that despite him describing the Nazi threat to Wojtek's family as an explanation for his spying activities, the security people saw it as nothing other than general background. He knew then that the system would swallow Wojtek and he would die, and probably sooner rather than later.

CHAPTER SIXTEEN

A few days later, the squadron's Spitfires were all at Deanland, after their transit from Coltishall. They were part of the force located at Aerodrome No. 149, fifteen miles from Brighton. Their flight south had been uneventful — no maintenance issues, no weather issues, and no sign of enemy aircraft. The absence of the Luftwaffe over England was becoming the norm. A good sign, in John's opinion. It confirmed the RAF had attained air superiority, at least over Britain.

Over the following weeks, 645 Squadron flew a lot of escort missions from Airfield 149, providing fighter cover for bombing missions. Early in May, John found himself assigned to lead a flight to escort an attack on some shipping that had been sighted in a port near Amsterdam. Six Spitfires were designated for fighter cover.

'We are to cover a low-level attack by Beaufighters,' John told the pilots who would be undertaking the mission with him. 'They are having a go at some vessels seen in Den Helder, about fifty miles north of Amsterdam, and will transit there not above two hundred feet. We will operate as three pairs, providing cover against any fighters and position two thousand yards behind the bombers, at their height, until we get close to target. Because they are going in low to avoid enemy radar detection, we must stay down too. Nevertheless, once we are four minutes out from target, we will go up to three thousand. I will call it as "*pop-up*" at the T minus four mark. I prefer to have a bit of height if we are going to get caught up with any enemy fighters as we arrive over the harbour where the target vessels are moored. I will lead that first pair, designated as Red

Section. Flight Lieutenant Edmonds, you lead the second pair, Yellow Section, and maintain one hundred and fifty yards behind me. Flight Lieutenant Giles, you take Green Section, one hundred and fifty behind Yellow. You are Yellow One and Green One respectively. You three —' he nodded towards the three pilots sitting behind Roger and Alistair — 'will be Red Two, Yellow Two, and Green Two.'

The three were new pilots, having joined the squadron in recent days, fresh from advanced air warfare training. Now they were to test their learning. John could not get over how young they appeared. *Could be bloody schoolboys*, he thought, before continuing.

'Each flight is to be echelon right off the pair leader, one hundred yards apart. Happy with that?'

'I would prefer a lesser lateral spacing, sir,' Roger replied. 'If we encounter enemy aircraft and operate in pairs, at least as long as we can, I like my wingman in close from the outset. Fifty yards would be good.'

John thought about that for a moment. 'Okay, let's do that. Fifty yards it is. We are to be airborne on the hour, to rendezvous over Norwich at one thousand feet. Because it's a low-level approach and attack, the Beaufighters intend to drop down to sea level after we cross the English coast, outbound. Their plan is to track directly to the Dutch seaside town of Ijmuiden, then turn north to Den Helder, about thirty miles along the coast from there. Anything else?'

There was nothing.

'Good-oh. Dispersal, ready to go at fifteen minutes before the hour. See you there.'

The Spitfires of 645 Squadron met the Beaufighters they were to escort just south of Norwich, and now they were all racing across the English Channel towards a planned landfall at

Ijmuiden. The bombers were a short distance ahead of the fighters, flying very close to the surface of the choppy grey sea. Initially, John had wondered why they didn't track directly to their target at Den Helder, rather than via Ijmuiden.

'If Jerry detects us on the way, he will be unsure of our target. Our route will look like an attack is planned on the northern areas of Amsterdam,' John had been told by the Officer Commanding Ops Planning when he had asked. 'Once we cross Ijmuiden, we turn away from our track towards Amsterdam and head north. It will only take us eight minutes to reach Den Helder from Ijmuiden. That reduces available reaction time for Jerry.'

Soon the British attackers were crossing the Dutch coast. Bang on track, John noted, as the small harbour at Ijmuiden flashed past below them. He rolled left, following the Beaufighters as they bore down on Den Helder, some thirty miles ahead of them.

With fifteen miles to run to target, four minutes at their current groundspeed, John made his climb call. In response to his transmission, the six Spitfires accompanying the Beaufighters all zoom-climbed to three thousand feet.

The area of the harbour where the target ships were moored was about a mile in from the mouth of a large estuary. As the bombers crossed the town, arrowing towards their targets, light anti-aircraft fire opened up. John could see small grey puffs in the air as shells exploded around the Beaufighters. Then there was a warning call from Red Two.

'Red One, enemy aircraft coming in, two o'clock high.'

John looked up to his right and saw them immediately. Nine fighters. *They look like Focke-Wulf 190s*, he decided. They were quick to respond, or maybe they were out anyway.

'All flights, engage at will, in your pairs,' John ordered.

The Germans were diving towards the Beaufighters, intent on stopping the bombing attack. The Spitfires all entered full-power climbs towards the approaching enemy aircraft. John was pleased they were starting from three thousand feet, and not from the close to ground-level height they had been a few moments ago. He fired a long burst at the leading Focke-Wulf. The Luftwaffe fighter veered away. *I must have scored a long-distance hit*, he thought, pleased to have disrupted its attack.

Within moments, the fighters of each side had closed in to a point where the engagement became a series of dogfights, marked by steep turns, rapid descents, and maximum-rate climbs. The pilots fought to outfly each other and gain a commanding position on the tail of their opponent. John got behind a German aircraft, which twisted and turned to get away, but without success. A burst from John's Spitfire sent the enemy aircraft tumbling from the sky. Another Focke-Wulf crossed in front of John, and he turned to follow. Just as he turned, there was an explosion close behind his cockpit.

He had not seen anyone coming. Looking over his shoulder, he saw one of the Germans was on his tail. There was no sign of his wingman, Red Two.

John rolled inverted and pulled into a vertical dive followed by a hard pull out and a steep turn to the left. Glancing behind, he saw his manoeuvring had shaken off his pursuer. He looked around and could see various dogfights going on, above and below him. Red Two was still nowhere in sight.

It looked as if at least half of the bombers had completed their attacks, and John was pleased to see four of the vessels that had been targeted were damaged, with two of them being consumed by large flames. Ack-ack fire around the port was intense, and several of the Beaufighters were hit. John increased power and dived towards the harbour's eastern seawall, on which he could see three anti-aircraft gun stations. Running along at one hundred feet above the seawall, John fired as he flew in towards the gun stations. The effect of his combined machine-gun fire and his two cannons was spectacular. The stations were savaged by the deadly hail that hit them, and even where not destroyed, no gun operator was left alive to continue firing.

John pulled up into a steep climb, eager to regain some altitude before re-engaging with the Focke-Wulfs. As he went through two thousand feet, he was desperately scanning for enemy aircraft. There was none to be seen. The fighter engagements were suddenly over, and no Luftwaffe aircraft were in sight. John had experienced it before. It was a strange feature of dogfighting — furious engagement to nothing, in an instant. Then he saw what he guessed was the last of the Beaufighters out over the estuary, turning west to head home. *Mission accomplished*, he thought. *Well done, chaps.*

'This is Red One, report in order, please,' John called on his radio. There was still nothing from Red Two, but he was delighted to hear the rest of his pilots check in.

Approaching the English coast, the Spitfires split away from the Beaufighters and made their way back to Airfield 149 at Deanland.

'Did anyone see what happened to Red Two?' John asked the others on the mission when they had landed. 'I had hoped he might be here when we got back, but there's no sign of him.'

No-one had seen Red Two, and John hated the uncertainty. It was bad enough to lose a pilot who had just joined the squadron and gone on his first war operation, but not knowing what had happened to him just compounded the loss.

John inspected his aircraft to see what had caused the huge bang behind his cockpit. When he saw the gaping hole in the fuselage, he understood. He had been hit by a cannon shell from one of the German aircraft. The armour plating behind his cockpit seat had saved his life.

'Big hole in your machine, sir,' Roger said to John as they walked back to the officers' mess after the debrief. 'Thank goodness for armour plating. Looks like you took a twenty-millimetre shell just behind where you were sitting. Too close for comfort.'

Early the next day, John was advised that the squadron was to escort some American Martin B-26 Marauders on their mission to bomb the railway junction at Valenciennes.

'It's an important point in the rail network, eighty miles east of Calais,' the ops controller said to him. 'The objective is to make internal transport difficult in France. We are doing everything we can to impede Germany's ability to move men and materials about.'

The controller did not say so, but John realised this must be a prelude to the impending invasion. *Jerry doesn't know where we will land our forces*, he thought. *If, consequently, they hold their reserves back from the coast, ready to be sent forward once it's clear where the Allies are coming ashore, we can make that movement difficult for them by disrupting the transport network.*

'Gentlemen, today we are escorting a bombing raid on the Valenciennes rail hub. It's a big raid. Seventy-six American B26s are involved.'

Roger whistled. 'Seventy-six! They must really want to knock the railway over.'

'Yes,' Alistair agreed. 'That's a lot of tonnage to be dropped.'

'It's all about wiping out the ability of German High Command to efficiently move their military forces to wherever the invasion occurs,' John responded. 'I can also tell you that I have been told we will be escorting a similar mission tomorrow, this time US Bostons — thirty-six of them, I understand, tasked with bombing the railway junction at Namur.'

'Is that in Belgium?' Roger asked.

'Yes, and it's only about ninety miles from Valenciennes, so, as you can see, there's a theme emerging. Railway junctions in the northern France, southern Belgium area.'

'Does that mean it's likely to be Pas de Calais where our forces go over, sir?'

'I don't know, but apparently they are both key transport junctions for German reserves held south of Brussels. Anyway, our brief is to rendezvous with the Marauders today at thirteen hundred hours, over Margate. They bomb from medium altitudes and have planned fourteen thousand feet for the Valenciennes railway raid. They will be airborne out of RAF Bury St Edmunds, up near Cambridge, so will be top of climb by the time they reach Margate. We will join them there, at that planned height, and proceed with them to target.'

'How many of our aircraft on this mission, sir?' asked Alistair.

'They want the full squadron on this one, so twelve. We will operate in three flights of four aircraft each.' John had always preferred a four-ship flight, operating the same way the Luftwaffe had operated their *schwarme* earlier in the war. As well as allowing a better lookout for enemy aircraft, it allowed an easy and efficient split into pairs. A lead Spitfire together with a wingman was John's favoured dogfighting configuration.

'Same as the Den Helder escort. I will lead Red Section, although on this sortie each section is four aircraft, not two. You, Flight Lieutenant Giles, take Yellow Section, and you, Flight Lieutenant Edmonds, take Green Section. Full squadron briefing in thirty minutes.'

The raid on the railway junction at Valenciennes went off perfectly. The weather played its part. Visibility was unimpeded, although there was soon a lot of smoke affecting what could be seen on the ground as the attack proceeded. The Germans sporadically fired some anti-aircraft rounds, but they exploded well off target, and none of the bombers was hit. *Where's the Luftwaffe?* John wondered. There was no sign of any enemy aircraft during the entire mission.

The next day, the raid on the Namur junction was not so successful. From his escorting Spitfire, John could see conditions were not favourable for accurate bombing, with a solid layer of cloud obscuring the target. The commander of the Boston bombers obviously thought the same. "Drop abandoned, return to base," was the call made by him when they were five minutes out from Namur.

Over following days, the full squadron escorted further bombing raids. First some Mitchells attacked the Lille railway junction, and then Bostons bombed the Douai junction to the south of Lille. Both raids were successful. John could see the extent of the destruction from the cockpit of his Spitfire as he circled over the bombers, ready to protect them from any Luftwaffe fighters that may appear. But none did. Some light flak was all that occurred, and while a few of the bombers were hit, no aircraft suffered any serious damage. John found himself wondering what had happened to the German defences.

'I can't understand what's going on with Jerry,' he said to his two flight commanders when they were sitting in the bar at the officers' mess, having completed their escort of the successful bombing mission over Douai. 'We've flown cover on three bombing raids in recent days, and no enemy aircraft have appeared.'

'Do you think they've been so badly hit in recent months that they don't have any adequate defensive capability left?' Roger asked.

'Maybe they're too committed on the Eastern Front, facing off against the Russians,' Alistair suggested.

'Whatever the reason, I don't mind,' John said with a smile. 'Suits me fine.'

A week later, near the end of May, John received orders that indicated a new approach. There were no bomber escort missions for 645 Squadron. Instead, the squadron was to carry out patrols over France, seeking out targets of opportunity. John assumed that meant the invasion was close and most key transport infrastructure had been destroyed. Now it was simple harassment of anything seen moving on the ground.

'If any of your pilots see trucks or staff cars moving about on the French roads, take them out. The trucks will be loaded with equipment or troops. The staff cars will carry commanders. Hitting them will be valuable at this point,' the war ops commander had briefed John.

To John, this signalled that the invasion was imminent.

'Change of approach from Command, gentlemen,' he said to Roger and Alistair. 'They aren't planning further bombing at present, so no escort duties for us. They want us to undertake Rhubarbs. We're to harass the Germans on the ground, hitting any transport and communication facilities we come across. Of course, if they launch fighters to intercept us, then we take them on. It's not just ground targets of opportunity. The intention behind this is to keep the German ground forces in a constant state of disarray. I think it also signals that the invasion will occur any day now.

'I propose that we run the Rhubarbs with flights of four aircraft. No need for a full squadron. That's not to say we will only operate that number of aircraft at any one time. There's no reason why we shouldn't get the whole squadron airborne and designate separate areas for each flight of four to cover.'

Roger and Alistair both agreed with that proposal.

The following morning, after a full briefing on the change of tactics, the squadron was airborne at ten hundred hours. John led Red Section. He was going to hunt for targets in an area centred on Lille. Alistair was to take his flight, Yellow Section, to patrol around Ypres. Meanwhile, Roger, with Green Section, would focus on an area centred on Arques.

Crossing the French coast just north of Boulogne-sur-Mer, John led his section east, towards Lille, about seventy-five miles ahead. Fifteen minutes into France, John saw a convoy of trucks on a road near Bethune. Ten plus, heading southwest.

'This is Red Leader. Truck convoy on the road ahead, Attacking. Follow me in line astern.'

They had been cruising at low level, four hundred feet above the terrain. John now dived lower, levelling at two hundred feet above the ground. He swept around in a steep turn as he approached the front of the convoy, following the line of the road. If the driver of the first vehicle saw the fast-approaching Spitfire, he gave no sign of it, maintaining a normal speed and direction. John fired. The salvo of machine-gun bullets and cannon shells tore into the front of the vehicle, which veered sharply off the road and tipped onto its side, before starting to burn. As John passed overhead, continuing to strafe the rest of the convoy, he was conscious of movement near the back of the truck he had just hit. Grey-coated German soldiers were jumping clear and running from the flames. *It's a troop convoy*, he thought. *Good.*

The remainder of John's section followed, all strafing in turn. As the four Spitfires departed the area, after making one run each, they left multiple wrecked trucks and a lot of enemy troops killed or wounded. It was a highly successful encounter, John decided.

After they had landed back at their base, John and his flight commanders met to discuss their respective missions. All had been successful. Roger's section had attacked some busy marshalling yards. As well as destroying railway wagons loaded with equipment, their shooting had caused a locomotive to blow up. The resulting explosion had been so large that number three in Roger's section, making a pass just as it occurred, had nearly been enveloped and brought down. A maximum-rate turn, to avoid the debris cloud rapidly growing in front of him, was all that had allowed the pilot and his aircraft to survive.

Alistair had also had success. He and his section had come across three staff cars, accompanied by motorcycles with sidecars. Those on the motorcycles appeared to be carrying machine guns, so they were clearly escorting high-value officers in the staff cars. All three cars were destroyed by the Spitfires that suddenly appeared, low and fast across the field next to the road. Those in the staff cars, and their guards, had no time to respond. The German occupying force in France lost some senior commanders in an instant.

'I have to say, independent sorties, prowling around the French countryside looking for targets, is a satisfying way to hit Jerry. It will keep them on edge. Nowhere is safe for them,' Alistair said with a grin. 'To be honest, I was surprised at the amount of satisfaction I got from destroying a German staff car. I knocked out some of the enemy's leadership capability there, so that's a good thing.'

'The cannons give us so much more punch than we had on the old Marks,' Roger commented. 'Eight machine guns on the earlier models was good enough during the dogfights of the Battle of Britain, but now we are attacking ground targets, give me the two cannons as well as some machine-gun capability. You can see the power. I doubt we would have blown up a locomotive with machine-gun fire alone.'

All three pilots nodded their agreement regarding the improved firepower of their Spitfire Mark Vs, with their combination of machine guns and cannons.

'What surprises me is that we still aren't seeing much of the Luftwaffe. Where are they?' Alistair asked.

'As well as being decimated when mounting their earlier attacks against Britain, they've lost men and machines on the Eastern Front. And don't forget Germany is being attacked night and day by RAF and US bombers, so they will be suffering supply issues. Fuel will be short. The factories manufacturing parts and equipment to keep their fighters airworthy are most likely suffering too. I can see why the Luftwaffe may not be up and about so much,' John said, 'but let's not drop our guard. They could appear anywhere at any time. We need to ensure we always remain alert in the air.'

Early the next day, John received a call from the war ops commander.

'Squadron Leader, we've just had a report regarding E-boat activity we want your squadron to check,' he said. 'Our bombers on their way to attack a factory near Tours called the sighting when they spotted what they think may have been E-boats, operating between the Cherbourg Peninsula and Le Havre. Get up as soon as you can, please, and see if you can locate any E-boats in that area.'

The squadron was on thirty-minute standby, but all twelve Spitfires were airborne within fifteen minutes. Flying at maximum continuous power, they were soon getting close to the French coastline. John could see the beaches of Normandy about ten miles ahead. He was leading six of the squadron's aircraft, approaching the search area from the direction of Cherbourg. Alistair was leading the other six Spitfires, coming in from the direction of Le Havre. They had split the squadron to cover the whole area more effectively. They were flying at three thousand feet — high enough to provide them with a good scanning altitude, and low enough to quickly dive in to attack anything seen below on the surface.

John saw them first: three E-boats, travelling at high speed by the look of the large foaming wakes they were creating on a relatively calm sea. He had heard they could reach speeds of about forty-five knots. They were all proceeding side by side, about two hundred yards apart.

'Three E-boats, travelling towards Le Havre on our eleven o'clock. Move to line astern in your pairs. I will take the most northerly boat together with my number two. Three and four, take the middle vessel. Five and six, you take the one closest to shore. Descending now to strafe from two hundred feet.'

As he called the attack profile, John hoped the crews on the E-boats had not seen them. *Good chance they haven't*, he thought. The Spitfires were coming in from behind, and the E-boats were cruising at high speed, so there was lots of engine and sea noise as they went.

Levelling at two hundred feet above the water, John prepared to fire. Out to his right he saw the other pairs were in a similar position, behind the E-boat they were to attack. When he was about eight hundred yards out, the vessel on which he was rapidly closing in started firing its rear deck gun. John began weaving and making slight height variations, trying to upset the German gunner's aim. He could see all the E-boats were now alerted, and tracer was flashing from them towards the other Spitfires.

A large flash and bang to his right caught John's attention. He was horrified to see Roger Edmonds' aircraft enveloped in flame, going down. In a matter of seconds, Roger's aircraft hit the water hard and disappeared in a cloud of spray. 'No!' John shouted. He knew Roger would have been killed. *Don't think about it right now*, he told himself, as he lined up the vessel in front of him and fired an extended burst of bullets and cannon shells. The result was spectacular and satisfying, given what had just happened to Roger. The E-boat exploded, and John pulled up steeply to avoid any debris.

'Bandits, ten plus, three o'clock high.' An urgent radio call from someone. John looked up to his right. Focke-Wulfs, which looked to be about six thousand feet above them, were diving down to attack.

'Break off from the boats. Engage the fighters at will,' John called, quickly lifting his Spitfire's nose and turning to meet the rapidly approaching Luftwaffe aircraft.

They have the height and speed advantage, John thought. As he watched, preparing to fire at the lead German, he saw two of the Focke-Wulfs begin to shed pieces of their fuselage and wings. The German pilots had not seen the six Spitfires led by

Alistair approaching them from the direction of Le Havre. The Focke-Wulfs abandoned their diving attack and scattered. Numerous dogfights followed, as the pilots of both sides manoeuvred to get a shot in the one-on-one encounters now occurring. It was over in ten minutes. None of the German aircraft had been downed, but neither had any of the Spitfires. There was damage to some, but nothing sufficient to bring them down. The Luftwaffe aircraft headed east into France, and John and his squadron turned back across the Channel to England.

Back on the ground at Deanland, the pilots were quiet and sombre. They all knew Roger Edmonds would have been killed when his Spitfire ploughed into the sea, out of control and at speed. Several of them had seen the incident that had cost Roger his life. At the mission debrief, John spoke to the pilots about the need to be steadfast. While he knew they were all feeling the loss of a squadron member, he assured them they would honour Roger by continuing to use their skills to defeat the enemy. 'Now is the time to press home the advantage being built,' he said. 'The Germans are suffering setbacks in a war that will soon be won, starting with the invasion of France any day now.'

John knew his men were all in mourning, but he was confident they would bounce back in short order. They had to.

CHAPTER SEVENTEEN

'Losing Roger is an absolute tragedy. He was such an integral part of the squadron's leadership. It's affecting everyone,' said Alistair quietly.

'Yes, it hurts,' John acknowledged, 'especially since we saw it happen. Hit in the fuel tank?'

'No,' Alistair replied. 'His number two said he took a cannon shell right in the nose area.'

'Wherever he was hit, it caused a catastrophic explosion. I saw his entire aircraft enveloped.'

'E-boats have a thirty-seven-millimetre flak cannon, sir. I think that's probably what it was. Unlucky shot, right in the front of the engine.'

'Yes, you may be right,' John agreed, before changing the subject. 'We are on bomber escort duties again, first thing tomorrow. Some Bostons are tasked with bombing the aerodrome at Evreux. That's about thirty miles south of Rouen. We are to rendezvous over Hastings at o-nine-hundred.'

Regular squadron life slowly resumed in the days following the loss of Roger. The pilots were kept so busy they did not have much time to dwell on what had happened to one of their flight leaders. As well as escorting the raid on Evreux aerodrome, they provided cover for some Mitchells bombing targets on the coast near Bayeux, and for some Bostons the following day, as they attacked rail infrastructure on the Belgian border. The only significant German resistance was on that border mission, where very heavy flak was encountered. Three of the Bostons were lost, but no Spitfire was hit. Once again, there was no sign of the Luftwaffe, which continued to surprise John.

John was working in his office early on the morning of the fifth of June, finishing his statistical report for May's war operations, when Group Captain Peter James came in.

'I have some news, Squadron Leader,' he said cheerily.

You're sounding pleased with the world, John thought to himself as he welcomed the group captain into his office.

'Look at this. It's on, tomorrow,' Peter said with a grin as he dropped a typewritten page in front of John. He picked it up and started to read:

SUPREME HEADQUARTERS ALLIED EXPEDITIONARY FORCE

Soldiers, Sailors, and Airman of the Allied Expeditionary Force!
You are about to embark upon the Great Crusade, toward which we have striven these many months. The eyes of the world are upon you. The hopes and prayers of liberty-loving people everywhere march with you. In company with our brave Allies and brothers-in-arms on other Fronts, you will bring about the destruction of the German war machine, the elimination of Nazi tyranny over the oppressed peoples of Europe, and security for ourselves in a free world.

John looked up, smiling. 'So, the invasion's about to begin?'

'Yes, our troops embark on their vessels to cross the Channel this afternoon, to land in France at first light. The invasion point chosen is Normandy.'

As he said that, John immediately thought of Roger, who had died in the waters off the Normandy beaches. With a pang of sadness, he replied, 'We've known it was coming, but we didn't know when or where.'

'I have the briefing for Six-four-five squadron. I will give it to you, and you can take it to your pilots later.'

'Certainly, sir. I'll just have a quick look at the remainder of this notice, to see if there is anything special that I need to be aware of.'

'There isn't. It's just a general notice being given to all personnel today. Nothing operational in it. Eisenhower is simply announcing the invasion and wishing everybody well.'

John quickly cast his eye over the remainder of the notice and nodded his agreement, noting the Allied supreme commander finished with an expression of good luck and support for what he was calling "*this great and noble undertaking.*"

'The task your squadron has been given, Squadron Leader, is to provide cover to the Americans as they come ashore. The invasion has been codenamed *Overlord.* This plan shows the actual beaches on which Allied forces will land,' Peter continued, as he laid out a large map showing the Normandy coast. 'As you can see, the beaches have been named Utah, Omaha, Gold, Juno, and Sword. You will operate over Utah and Omaha.'

John pored over the map as the group captain continued.

'British and US paratroopers are going to be put onto the Cherbourg Peninsula near Utah beach at first light. You are to be over your beaches at the same time, so that's airborne out of here at o-four-thirty. There will be some gliders coming later. Keep an eye out for them. You should be advised when they are due in. Basically, your job is to keep Jerry out of the sky over the beaches under your watch, and to give cover to the paratroops nearby, on Cherbourg. You may be asked to assist with any ground strikes needed, but that's uncertain at this point. There will be another squadron of Spitfires to assist you if Jerry turns up in numbers, but they won't be over the landing zones with you, unless it becomes necessary. The plan is for them to hold at sixteen thousand, about ten miles offshore, ready to join you if required. They can be with you in minutes if needed. Their callsign is "Intervener One." Yours is "Utah-Omaha Cover."'

'Right, we can do that, sir. It's a great step that's being taken tomorrow. Hopefully it all goes well.'

'The general view is that while there may be significant losses, we should get sufficient of our forces ashore to establish a beachhead from which we can build. If successful, and I'm confident we will be, it's the beginning of the end for Herr Hitler and his thugs. The Russians are making good headway against the Germans on the Eastern Fronts too, so it's just a matter of time until this is all over, thank God. By the way, invasion day, the sixth of June, is being called D-Day.'

After the group captain had gone, John sat thinking about what he had just been told and began planning the way the squadron would operate to achieve the objectives set. He decided he would split the squadron in two.

Six aircraft would operate at a lower level, around three thousand feet, tasked with confronting any enemy aircraft flying low around the beaches, and assisting suppression of any point that ground forces found difficult to approach. Those six aircraft would patrol the length of Utah and Omaha, just seaward of the waterline, flying up and down a line that paralleled the shore. The other six Spitfires would be at fourteen thousand feet, flying an extended race-track pattern at that altitude. One side of the pattern would be a mile out to sea, the other side about a mile inland. That position and pattern would provide the upper group with a good overview of the area, and enable early sighting of any enemy aircraft approaching, whether over Utah or Omaha, or the paratroops on the peninsula. Fourteen thousand feet would be a useful height for interception of medium to higher altitude Luftwaffe aircraft.

'Looks fine to me, sir,' Alistair said after John had briefed him on what he had been told by Peter, and how he planned 645 Squadron would meet the requirement to provide air cover.

'Okay, let's get the chaps in and brief them.'

Before first light the next morning, D-Day, twelve Spitfires of 645 Squadron sat at dispersal, engines grumbling. They were fully fuelled and armed. The squadron's maintenance fitters had worked through the night, checking and rechecking the aircrafts' systems and gear. No-one wanted to have to have one of their Spitfires drop out of the invasion as the result of some malfunction.

Alistair was flight commander for Yellow Section, comprising the six aircraft that would operate at an upper level. John was leading the six-ship Red Section, tasked with covering the landing areas at a lower level, patrolling at three thousand feet. All the pilots had been thoroughly briefed and were ready.

Climbing out of Deanland, or Aerodrome No. 149 as it was known for invasion-planning purposes, the squadron flew in the early morning darkness towards France. They planned to stop their climb at eight thousand feet, and to stay together until twenty miles out from the Normandy coast. Then the lower-level patrol would begin its descent to its planned height of three thousand, and the top cover would climb to fourteen thousand feet. After fifteen minutes, as the sun started to come up over the horizon far ahead of them, day slowly replaced night. When John looked down, he was amazed. There were ships everywhere — hundreds of them — carrying troops towards France. *What a sight*, he thought.

'Twenty miles. Yellow Section, climb to establish overhead pattern at fourteen thousand,' John called on his radio. 'Report established. Red Section, descending now to three thousand.'

'Wilco, Red Leader,' Alistair called as his section began climbing towards its initial position high over Utah and Omaha beaches, at the western end of the Allied landing areas.

Soon, John's section was at three thousand feet, directly over Omaha beach, with a grandstand view of the invasion.

'Yellow Section established,' Alistair called a few minutes later.

John acknowledged that call and then instructed his own section to form three pairs, each pair flying two hundred yards behind the other, as they had discussed at the pre-mission briefing. All the pilots were scanning the area, searching for any sign of the Luftwaffe. There was nothing to be seen. Twenty minutes passed — still no German aircraft. Below, they could see the landing craft dropping troops into the surf, just off the sandy beaches. John could not help comparing the situation now with how it had been over the Dunkirk beaches when the British Expeditionary Force was evacuating from France, under enormous German pressure. Then, wave after wave of Luftwaffe bombers had come over, trying to destroy the thousands of soldiers horribly exposed below. John and his fellow fighter pilots had fought tenaciously to stop them. But this morning, over the Normandy beaches, John realised the Luftwaffe was not coming. *They don't have the aerial capacity they once had*, John decided. *That's very good for the thousands of troops swarming ashore down there.*

After another thirty minutes over the landing beaches designated Utah and Omaha, John knew it was time to go back to Deanland. Their presence was limited by their fuel endurance, and it was now time to return to base. A fresh squadron would take their place, protecting the landings from German air attack.

'Utah-Omaha air cover, this patrol is complete. Return to base,' John instructed with a call on his radio.

While their aircraft were being refuelled and checked, the squadron pilots gathered in the dispersal area. No re-arming was required. Not a shot had been fired by any one of the Spitfires.

John could feel the air of excitement among the pilots, not just because the long-anticipated invasion was finally underway, and appeared to be going well, but because they had all just seen an amazing sight. Below them, hundreds of ships had been crossing the English Channel together, taking their precious cargoes of men and equipment to Normandy. Closer to the shore itself, they had seen the many landing craft buffeting their way through the coastal waves, before dropping their flat, flap-like frontal area to allow the soldiers they were carrying to charge ashore. John had seen the troops running up the beach, towards the positions where German defenders sat waiting and shooting. The whole thing was not a sight easily forgotten.

'Gentlemen,' John called, standing on an empty ammunition box as he spoke to the assembled pilots, 'that went well, both from our perspective, and hopefully, for those on the ground. No Luftwaffe seen.' There was a murmur of agreement from the pilots. John continued, 'I have just received a copy of a preliminary invasion report from Allied Command. I've pinned it on the noticeboard in the ops room so you can all have a look.

'We are to go out again at o-eight-thirty hours. Do whatever you need to do now, so you will be ready to take off at that time. Same area for our next patrol — Utah and Omaha beaches — and same procedures: upper patrol by Yellow Section, lower patrol by Red. There will be a reserve squadron holding over the Channel, again, ready to come in if we spot the Hun approaching the landing areas. Any questions?'

'Yes, sir,' a young, sandy-haired pilot standing at the back called. 'Where do you think Jerry has gone? Unusual not to see a single enemy aircraft over France.'

'Well, the Luftwaffe's aeronautical infrastructure and support networks have been the subject of a lot of attention from Bomber Command in recent months, with direct attacks on aerodromes in France. That will have affected capacity. Also, the fact the landings occurred in Normandy may have caught the Germans by surprise. Nevertheless, they will reorganise and regroup, so we should expect the Luftwaffe at some point. Any more questions?' No-one else raised their hand. 'Okay, if there's nothing else, be back here soon for departure.'

Several of the pilots headed to the operations room, wanting to see the initial report from Allied Command. John looked in briefly as they clustered around the noticeboard, reading the report on the invasion's progress. It said:

0735 hours. 6th June.

BRITISH AIRBORNE OPERATIONS: –
374 a/c operated – 8 missing – 10 gliders aborted – 2 parachutes aborted

U.S. AIRBORNE OPERATIONS: –
821 a/c operated with 103 gliders – 21 a/c missing, 4 gliders aborted.

No enemy air reaction.

The second patrol by 645 Squadron was very similar to the first. No Luftwaffe aircraft appeared, although the squadron was asked to orbit for ten minutes as it first approached the French coastline. Some Royal Navy vessels, standing some miles off the coast, were undertaking a massive bombardment of German defences established behind the beaches, about two thousand yards inland.

'Don't want any of our shells going through one of your aeroplanes flying around in that area,' the naval officer calling via the special surface-to-air frequency had joked. 'We will be complete at o-nine-hundred, then you can go in, but hold west of us in the meantime. I will call you to confirm when we have finished.'

That confirmation had come ten minutes later, as anticipated, and the Spitfires were soon established on patrol over Utah and Omaha beaches. John could see huge fires and large columns of smoke rising from the remains of whatever structures had been there before the naval bombardment. Whatever it was, whoever it was, they had no chance against the big naval guns, he thought. This was firepower at its best, supporting the ground forces.

The squadron's third and final D-Day patrol had them airborne out of Deanland at 1730 hours. John was surprised at the time they had on the ground between their second and third patrols, but realised there would be a reason. The comprehensive planning undertaken by Allied Command would ensure squadrons were used effectively, and that there were no gaps in the air cover over the beaches of Normandy.

Once again, on the third patrol, there was no sign of any Luftwaffe aircraft over the invasion landing area, but John and his section did get the opportunity to fire their guns on this occasion. A call on the surface-to-air frequency was made by a ground force commander at Omaha beach soon after they had arrived overhead to begin patrolling.

'We have a mortar nest, with supporting machine guns, well established in a small commune about eight hundred yards beyond the seawall at the eastern end of the Omaha landing area. The commune comprises a single row of twelve two-storey houses sited along the southern side of the only road there. The properties where Jerry has set up are the last three houses at the western end of that row. Are you able to take them out? They have had us pinned down for hours, and the navy can't help with its big guns as they are replenishing ammunition and aren't programmed to shell again until the morning. We would like to deal with these chaps now, if you can assist?'

'We can do that,' John replied. 'We will reposition and call back in a moment. I will use Spitfire Red One as my call-sign.' He called his section on the air-to-air frequency. 'Red Section, Red One. We've had a request from the ground force controller on Omaha. He wants us to take out some mortars and machine guns set up in three houses in a commune a short distance in from the landing area. I'm going to make a pass to familiarise myself. I will fly over the centre property of the three to identify our targets. Position to observe me from a safe area beyond the breakers. Watch the track I take and the house I cross. That will confirm what we are to attack — that house, and the one on either side of it. They are the three houses at the western end of the row.'

Then he called the ground force commander again.

'Ground Commander, this is Spitfire Red One. One aircraft is going to make a low pass over the houses you have identified, so you can confirm we are targeting the correct buildings.'

John left the others orbiting a short distance out to sea, then dived towards the shore, airspeed building rapidly. He had identified the commune while further out. There was only one commune at Omaha with nothing other than a single row of twelve houses. He wanted to be low and fast as he went over. He would be a difficult target for any German gunner in front of him, to say nothing of any panicking Allied troops who might shoot at anything passing overhead, unsure if it was friend or foe. He realised the special "invasion stripes" painted on the wings of Allied aircraft, including his squadron's Spitfires, may not guarantee there would be no friendly fire directed at him.

John was at two hundred feet and three hundred and thirty miles per hour as he flashed across the beach, over the seawall, and then up and over the last three houses in the row. A stream of tracer flashing past his cockpit told him where at least one of the enemy machine guns was situated. He entered a climbing turn to the right, coming back around through one hundred and eighty degrees to head back to his section.

'Ground Commander, Spitfire Red One. You will have seen where I passed over the houses. I drew fire from the end house. Confirm I have identified the correct targets.'

'Affirmative. The house you flew over is the centre property of the three to be attacked.'

'Roger, we will run in shortly.'

Back on the air-to-air frequency, John called the others in Red Section.

'You saw my track. Those last three houses in the row of homes at the western end of the commune are confirmed as our targets. I will take the third property from the end, with Red Two. Red Three, you and Red Four take the house second from the end — that's the one I crossed. Red Five, with Red Six, the last property in the row is your target. You are shooting at any pits you see in front of your target property, and machine guns are established on their first floors. Let's go — three-hundred-yard intervals between each of the attacking pairs.'

John rolled his Spitfire towards the shoreline, and with Red Two just behind him and twenty yards out to his right, both aircraft accelerated towards the houses in the beachside commune in which the Germans had established themselves. The other Spitfires tasked with the attack would follow, in turn, at three-hundred-yard spacings from the two Spitfires in front of them, targeting their designated houses.

Their engines were howling under full power. Crossing the area separating the commune from Omaha beach, John began firing. He saw the combination of his cannon shells and machine-gun bullets rip and shred the bunker the German mortar crew had set up there. Then the windows in the house exploded as he lifted his line of fire slightly. A large wooden front door disintegrated into a splintered mess. Dust belched from the property as its insides were penetrated and destroyed by the heavy fire. Walls crumbled and grass and earth flew as fire from Red Two added to the conflagration. Red Two had unleashed a similar barrage against the German strongpoint. John knew that no German mortar shell or machine-gun fire would come from that house again.

The scene was replicated by the following Spitfires of Red Section, as each of the remaining target houses were obliterated in turn by the concentrated fire.

'Thank you, Spitfires,' the ground commander said, when John called him to confirm all that was required had been done. 'I saw what you did, and my people on scene tell me the threat has been removed. Good work.'

'My pleasure,' John replied. 'We will resume air defence patrol.'

Over the following days, John and his squadron flew two or three air-cover sorties every day. He had been amazed by the number of parachutes he saw lying on the ground further inland. *Literally thousands*, he thought. *That's a lot of paratroopers coming in; the Germans must have wondered how they would be able to successfully repel so many Allied troops on D-Day.* He had seen how they had poured onto the beaches from their landing craft, and he realised they must have tumbled out of the sky in their parachutes in huge numbers, as well. Then, the Germans would have been confronted with hundreds of gliders arriving swiftly and quietly, carrying yet more Allied soldiers.

Many of the gliders had obviously had a difficult landing, judging by the number of wrecked hulks John saw lying in almost every field in the area, but the soldiers inside must have been okay. The initial report from Allied Command had reported only fourteen gliders aborted, between both the British and Americans. There were more than fourteen wrecks, so John decided "aborted" must have meant they did not even make it to Normandy, or were destroyed on arrival, along with their occupants.

By day three of the invasion, the eighth of June, it became clear the Allied forces were making good progress, with some troops penetrating several miles into France beyond the Normandy beaches. Despite the poor weather conditions that day, John and his squadron members could see the Allied columns moving inland. For the first time, he started thinking that the war would be over very soon.

CHAPTER EIGHTEEN

'You've spent the last four days providing air cover over your allocated landing areas,' Peter said to John when he was back at base, 'and now Command wants Six-four-five to extend its operations. The beachheads are secure, so you are to operate further inland. Also, there is a special op planned, further west.'

'What's that, sir?' John asked.

'You are to run a low-level sortie over the Cherbourg Peninsula. This is a reconnaissance mission. Command is keen to get some idea of Luftwaffe strength around Cherbourg. The thinking is that if we send a couple of Spits into the area to have a look, that will help us confirm Jerry's aircraft dispositions. It might also stimulate a response from any German fighters based there. That will enable us to see what Jerry has in the area.'

'We are bait?'

'I wouldn't put it like that, but we have noted the Luftwaffe's absence over the landing areas in Normandy, and we want to find out where they are and what they're doing. A reconnaissance mission will help us gauge Luftwaffe strength on the peninsula. The port at Cherbourg is an important facility for the Allied forces. They want control of the port as soon as possible. A rapid advance towards that port is planned, but no-one is sure of the enemy's aerial strength in there. Your reports, whether from observation or engagement, perhaps both, will give us the answer.'

'Passing Pointe des Groins,' John called as he and Alistair swept past the north-western tip of the Cherbourg Peninsula, fast and low. He followed that call a few minutes later with a heading change: 'Left thirty.'

The two Spitfires banked to the left, crossing the low cliffs near Goury, to track across the peninsula. Utah beach was fifty-four miles ahead, on the other side of the peninsula. Both pilots were scanning carefully, looking for aircraft on the ground as well as in the air as they raced across the French countryside, no more than five hundred feet above the terrain.

'I see an aerodrome to our west, with what looks like a substantial number of multi-engine aircraft parked around its perimeter,' John called on his radio to Alistair. 'See them?'

'No, but I do see ten plus bandits on our nine o'clock. Estimate three thousand feet. They've seen us. One-o-nines. And more,' Alistair added grimly, 'this time on our one o'clock. Six of them. Focke-Wulfs.'

'Let's get out of here,' John called. 'Full-power climb. We'll get into the cloud to the east. That will hide us, then we'll turn for home. There's too many of them.'

When John was back on the ground at Deanland, he went straight to Peter to complete his debriefing. 'Not so sure about that tactic, sir,' John said.

'It had to be done, Squadron Leader. It's a priority to take the harbour at Cherbourg. That's why Utah beach was added as a landing area late in the invasion planning and paratroopers were put onto the peninsula nearby. We wanted additional troops at the western end of the invasion beaches, ready to go on to Cherbourg in short order. The temporary Mulberry harbours are okay, but they were never going to be anything but a short-term solution with the changeable weather and sea conditions expected in that area. What you found today is valuable in helping us assess the German air defences in the area.'

'Two aircraft deliberately flying into what was always going to be a well-defended area, given the importance of the port at Cherbourg, to gauge air-defence response, is not optimum in my view, sir. We were lucky we got away. We had more than sixteen of the blighters coming at us from different directions. It might have been better to have sent a high-level specialist recon flight over.'

'I'm sorry, Squadron Leader; those were the orders. I'm pleased you got back safely. We now know there's a considerable Luftwaffe fighter and bomber presence there, sited at different aerodromes nearer to Cherbourg. I think Bomber Command is going in to attack all the airfields in the area now we know that for sure. They will of course take an escort with them.'

John's squadron was not asked to escort the bombing raids over the Cherbourg Peninsula that followed over subsequent days, but those raids must have achieved their objectives. The Allies captured their coveted deep-water port two weeks later, largely unhindered by any attacks by the Luftwaffe. In the meantime, John and his squadron had taken their air cover patrols further into France, protecting troops moving towards Tours, and the prize of Paris.

At the beginning of July, 645 Squadron was re-equipped. The Spitfire Vs were replaced with Spitfire IXs. It meant higher-powered Merlin engines, additional fuel capacity, and an improved rate of climb.

'These will be good,' John said to Alistair when the Mark Ixs arrived. John had just test-flown one of them. 'Four hundred plus at altitude. That's ten per cent faster than the fives, and they go up like a rocket.'

Alistair just smiled at John's enthusiasm.

'Tomorrow morning, early, there's a big do planned for Scrignac, a small village on the Brest Peninsula, forty miles east of Brest itself,' Peter told John one afternoon, soon after the squadron had received the new aircraft. 'We're going in with four waves of twelve Spitfires each, loaded with bombs for the attack. A five-hundred-pounder on the centre rack, and two-hundred-and-fifties under each wing. You are to lead the second wave.'

John was surprised. It was unusual to mount such a large-scale bombing raid with Spitfires, forty-eight of them delivering a thousand pounds of high explosive each. And the target — a French village? *What about the civilians there?* He wondered.

'Do we know why Scrignac is the target? And what about the local populace? That sort of attack will obliterate a small village.'

'Of course, I was coming to that. The residents have been moved out by the Germans, who have set up a regional command base in the village. The houses are now all occupied by the troops garrisoned there. It's effectively a German town in France, and importantly, it's a command-and-control centre for their operations in that area.'

John nodded his acknowledgement as the group captain continued.

'Airborne time is o-seven-hundred. Briefing for all squadrons involved is o-six-hundred. Latest intelligence on defences will be available then, together with current weather en route and at the target.'

*

Next morning, as the Spitfires swept in low over the French coastline, near Lannion on the Brest Peninsula, the morning sky was clear and there were no enemy aircraft to be seen. There was some light flak from time to time, but it was inaccurate and ineffective. Within minutes the target village, Scrignac, was dead ahead. The Germans were caught totally unaware. The flak in the town did not start until the first wave was almost overhead, and there were no Luftwaffe defenders. The first Spitfires dropped their bombs. One minute behind, John, leading the second wave, descended to treetop height and increased power His target area was the central square area of the village.

As he climbed following bomb release, and turned back towards the Channel John could see many of the buildings in the village had been badly damaged. Dust, mixed with smoke, swirled everywhere. He also noted the flak guns had fallen silent. There were no more tell-tale ack-ack puffs in the air.

Back on the base, as he finished the operational debrief, Peter said, 'Scrignac no longer exists. The only building reported as still standing is the village church. We had no losses. So well done everybody.'

'The place was well and truly pranged,' John said to Alistair as they left at the conclusion of the meeting.

'Yes, that's one Nazi command-and-control centre that won't be doing any more work. I feel a bit sorry for the folk who used to live there. They'll have nothing to come back to once Jerry is pushed out of the area. Nearly every building is flattened.'

'That's war, I'm afraid,' John responded. 'Lots of people are not going to have a home when it's all over, in Britain and throughout Europe, to say nothing of what's happening in Asia with the Japanese. And look at the carnage in North Africa. This is truly a world war. I suppose if you're still alive at the end of it, that's a bonus.'

'Very philosophical, Squadron Leader,' said Peter, who had come up behind them.

'With the times we live in, sir, we need to be philosophical to keep going. But I have to say, it does seem to be getting easier. Jerry is mostly on the back foot these days.'

'Indeed, Squadron Leader. Things are changing now, and quite rapidly. Could you come and see me before dinner this evening? Say, six, in my office?'

'Squadron Leader,' Peter said, when he met with John as arranged, 'you are going to be posted to an outfit operating in Norfolk, the Central Fighter Establishment. Your role will be to undertake a review of general operational practices and fighter tactics put in place for a new aircraft.'

John was stunned. He was going from being Commanding Officer of 645 Squadron, leading his Spitfires on various missions over Western Europe, to reviewing operational practices and tactics at some new squadron? 'I don't understand, sir,' was all he could manage.

'You are coming off war ops because we have surplus fighter capacity at present, especially now the Americans are here with their P51s, and this conflict is rapidly concluding. It will be over inside eight months, mark my words.'

'With respect, sir, I understand that, but if the RAF is going to begin reducing its operational fighter capacity because it expects the war to end soon, I would have thought the reduction might start at the other end of the spectrum. Not with the more experienced pilots who are currently leading the squadrons.'

'Ah, don't misunderstand this, Squadron Leader. You have been selected because of your experience and operational skill. That's what's going to be needed where you are going.'

'Where is that?'

'You will be aware Britain has recently developed jet-powered fighters?'

'I am. The Gloster Meteor, but while there is an operational squadron, I understand use of the aircraft is very limited. Nothing to be flown over enemy territory.'

'Correct. We don't want one shot down and falling into German hands. But its use is not restricted just for that reason. We still have a lot to learn about jet operations and how best to use those aircraft in combat. Currently, the Meteors spend most of their time chasing down V-bombs. There has been a lot of work done on operational use of the jets by a team based at Farnborough. But those in charge at Command now want that work stepped up. There's no suggestion that what we have now on jets is not up to standard. They just want to ensure everything is optimum, and they think a follow-up review is the best way to do that.

'However, there is more to your posting than reviewing jet tactics and use. While a review will be useful, Command wants three experienced and capable fighter pilots with leadership experience not only to have a second look at tactics, but also to develop a demonstration flight programme. You fit the bill perfectly: a successful and experienced fighter pilot. Exactly the sort of person Fighter Command wants to help the RAF move to its next phase with jet fighters, and, it seems, to help market the Meteor on behalf of Britain by demonstrating its war capabilities to our allies once the fighting is over.'

John appreciated that what he was being asked to do was something special, but it had caught him by surprise. He just nodded his acknowledgement.

'You will be going to RAF West Raynham, in Norfolk, to take up this new role. You are to be there by the beginning of November.'

At least I get a few more of months leading my squadron, John thought. *After that, the war will be unexpectedly over for me.*

'Very well, sir, I understand the imperatives behind this. Who will take over Six-four-five?' he asked.

'Flight Lieutenant Giles will be promoted to Squadron Leader, and he will assume your CO responsibilities once you go.'

John was happy with that. As well as being a capable fighter pilot, Alistair would be a good leader.

'The adjutant will be in touch regarding transfer arrangements in due course. Thank you, Squadron Leader. I know your contribution will be valuable to the new jet programme, and keep this under your hat in the meantime, please. Everyone at Command is a bit sensitive about confidentiality on jets.'

With that, the meeting was over, and John, still feeling the surprise, made his way back to the officers' mess for dinner.

Over the following months, John found himself flying a range of missions. Often, he was part of an escort to bombers taking out key infrastructure targets in France, and sometimes he was just on offensive patrols, looking for targets of opportunity. Occasionally, Luftwaffe fighters would appear, but the attempts at intervention by small groups of Me 109s or FW 190s were never going to pose a serious threat to the hundreds of Allied aircraft now regularly mounting attacks throughout

Western Europe. German forces, whether in the air or on the ground, were continually on the back foot. John realised that Peter had been right. The war would be over very soon.

In his last few days before he was due to move to his new role on jets, John was leading the squadron on a long-range patrol, covering an area north-east of Brussels. The Allied ground forces had surged through France and into Belgium in recent weeks, but had been slowed up by fierce German resistance around Antwerp. John's brief for this patrol was to look out for, and attack, any enemy troops seen moving in the area. There was little flak being encountered by the patrol, just the occasional round when they passed near something the Germans must have decided warranted some ground defence. There were not many such sites. No enemy aircraft were engaged. Some fighters were sighted nearby, but when the squadron turned towards them, the Luftwaffe aircraft headed for nearby cloud cover and disappeared.

'Nothing doing, lads. Set a heading for home,' John called as he rolled his aircraft into a turn for the others to follow, disappointed they had not seen any targets on the ground.

Halfway through the turn, Alistair called, 'Red Leader, this is Yellow One. Thought I saw movement in the woods on our starboard side.'

John looked down to his right. They were flying at three thousand feet. 'Don't see anything,' he replied, 'but orbit here and I will go down and have a closer look.'

John peeled away and dived towards the woods below. He levelled his aircraft at what he estimated was one hundred feet above the trees and throttled back his engine to make a slow pass overhead whatever it was that Alistair thought he might have seen. As he traversed the woods, he rolled his Spitfire gently from side to side, peering down through the foliage.

Problem is, John thought, *I can't see through the tree canopy. There would be camouflage netting as well, I guess, if Jerry's hiding in there*. He decided to have one last look from minimum altitude. If he could not see down through the trees, he would peer under them.

John descended towards the west, away from the woodland area, and then turned and flew directly back towards the woods at fifty feet above the ground. Three hundred yards from the treeline, he saw flashes in the shadow created by the relatively dense foliage. *What's that? Christ, someone's shooting at me!* he thought. Then he saw what had been impossible to see looking down through the trees: a line of parked vehicles. There were tanks, trucks, and half-track carriers lined up, obviously trying to remain hidden under the tree canopy from any searching eyes in the sky. He heard and felt some of the fire being directed towards him hitting his aircraft. Pieces flew off his left wing. John hauled back on his control column and applied full power, quickly zooming up above the treetops and out of the line of fire.

'This is Red Leader,' John called to the squadron orbiting higher overhead. 'There's a mechanised column hidden in the trees. We will position one mile west of the woods and run in low, not above one hundred feet, to strafe them. You will see Jerry is parked under the trees as you approach. They're in a line that must be half a mile long, given the number of vehicles I saw. The line runs from north to south. There's a white farmhouse sitting by itself at the one west point. That's opposite the midpoint of the line, so use that as your marker. I will lead the attack, commencing my run-in from above that farmhouse. Red and Yellow Sections, echelon left on me, at fifty-yard spacing. Blue and Green Sections, echelon right on me, same spacing.'

As the Spitfires swooped in, John could see the Germans were firing furiously with everything they had. Gun flashes could be seen along the full length of the line of parked vehicles. The soldiers there, hoping they would be hidden from the air, had realised they had been discovered. But they had no chance against twelve Spitfires. Each aircraft had two cannons, delivering deadly 20mm shells, and four machine guns, spraying .303 calibre bullets. The result was inevitable. Under the hail of fire delivered by the Spitfires as they flew low across the field, many German soldiers died, and most of their machines were damaged or destroyed.

On John's last night at Deanland with 645 Squadron, the pilots decided they would say farewell to their commanding officer in style. The mess sergeant had been persuaded to acquire some good meat to go with the vegetables sourced from various gardens near the aerodrome. It was a miracle dinner, given the rationing restrictions.

'Squadron Leader, you go with our kindest wishes and fondest memories,' Alistair said as he concluded his short speech, during which he had reminded everyone of John's contribution, both as a leader and as an operational pilot. 'He hasn't told us exactly where he's going or what he's planning to do, but I'm assured it has nothing to do with a woman.'

There was a lot of laughter from the assembled pilots. John grinned sheepishly, pushing any thought of Mary out of his head.

'Maybe I can just say it's life in the fast lane for you now — very fast, I think,' Alistair continued. More laughter. While no-one was sure, they had all heard the rumour that John had been selected to help the RAF develop its jet fighter operations. 'It's my pleasure to present you with this small token, suitably inscribed so you will always think of us whenever you use it.' Alistair handed John a large silver cup, to the applause of the watching pilots.

'Thank you, Squadron Leader Giles, and congratulations on your promotion and being given command of this wonderful squadron,' John said, eyeing the cup, which was engraved: *To The Fieriest Ferkin, alias Squadron Leader John Noble.* 'I'm not sure why I'm described as fiery. Thought I was the calm type.'

That caused hoots of laughter.

'And I'm not even going to ask what a "Ferkin" is,' he continued. 'I will just say this. I have enjoyed my time as your CO. You are a capable group and you are all good people personally. It has been my pleasure to be associated with you all. Thank you.'

That night, John wrote to his parents, telling them his role in war operations had finished and he was being assigned to a new development role in the RAF. He didn't say what that role was, being conscious of the security around the Meteors, but he knew his parents would be thankful he was no longer actively engaged in the fighting.

Better get packed and organised, he decided, looking around his office and thinking about his personal belongings back in his room, all soon to be put into his large leather suitcase for the road trip to RAF West Raynham.

CHAPTER NINETEEN

John discovered RAF West Raynham was a relatively new station, constructed five years previously. He had not been familiar with the aerodrome, so he had undertaken some research to find out what he could.

West Raynham had two concrete runways. One was 5,800 feet long, the other, 4,350 feet. John knew the length was necessary for jet operations. The runways had been constructed in late 1943, to replace the existing grass operational areas. The longer runway vector was orientated northeast/southwest, while the slightly shorter one ran east/west.

On arrival, John and the two other pilots who had been selected to join the Central Fighter Establishment were greeted by Wing Commander David Hill.

'Gentlemen, welcome to West Raynham,' he said, looking at each of them in turn.

The two other pilots alongside John were Squadron Leaders Jack Piper and Ken Smiley. Jack Piper was an experienced pilot who had flown Spitfires right through the war, since 1939. Ken Smiley was one of the pilots from the RAF squadron that had already been operating the Meteor on a limited basis, since mid-1944.

'You have ahead of you two incredibly important tasks. First, reviewing the tactical and operational arrangements established to date for the Meteor, to allow the development of any further air warfare techniques. Second, when the war is over, undertaking the demonstration of the aircraft to various interested parties.

'We've had the Meteor operating for some time now, and that's long enough to tell us we need to review our current procedures for use in jet operations. Those procedures were developed initially at Farnborough, by a specialist group, but there are some operational issues emerging, and further strategic and tactical matters we want addressed on this new type. You are here because you are considered to be among the best fighter pilots we have, and we are going to use your skills and experience to ensure we get the most out of our new aircraft.'

Hill paused as the three pilots nodded their understanding.

'Apart from Squadron Leader Smiley, you haven't flown jets, so there's a bit of learning ahead of you. Ground-school classes start tomorrow, o-eight-thirty hours in this room. The initial focus will be the theory and procedures for jet engines generally, the systems in the Meteor, and the standard operating procedures we use in that aircraft. Squadron Leader Smiley, you need not attend these initial classes, given you are already rated and have some operational experience on the Meteor.'

Ken Smiley acknowledged this with another nod.

'After completion of that initial phase of ground school, the focus will be on flying the Meteor. There will be oversight here from one of our pilots involved in initial test-flying and operational-use development at Farnborough. He will join us for a few days and brief you on his experience in the aircraft and discuss things you need to be alert for in the air. Then it will be the first jet solos for Squadron Leaders Piper and Noble, followed by a programme of consolidation flying so there is complete familiarity with the aircraft and its performance. You will also be involved in this part of the programme, Squadron Leader Smiley.'

'Is that necessary, sir?' he responded. 'I've already had some months on limited war ops in the Meteor back at my squadron.'

'We think it is necessary. All three of you should undertake the same flying programme, so that together, as the development team, you have a common approach to all the operational matters we want to explore with this aircraft.'

'Very well, sir,' Ken agreed, but it was clear from his tone that he felt he should not be required to join that part of the programme, either.

Over the following weeks, the team made good progress. The two newcomers to jet operations settled into the aircraft well and were soon flying the Meteor with precision and accuracy in all its flight regimes. Once the flying exercises reached a more advanced stage, Ken joined John and Jack in the flying operations being undertaken. Despite his experience and self-confidence, Ken was not flying the Meteor with the same level of precision and competence as John and Jack. On one occasion, he failed to reduce his speed adequately for his landing approach. Consequently, he touched down much too fast, and too far along the runway. He was very near the end of the runway before he managed to get the Meteor airborne again, after aborting his attempt to land. The risk of an over-run had been substantial.

That incident should have reminded Ken of some important principles of jet operation, but he did not want to discuss it or even acknowledge he had made a mistake. Two mistakes really, so far as John was concerned: failing to actively manage speed when on descent to land, and failing to appreciate that instant thrust, unlike a reciprocating engine driving a propellor, was not available from a jet engine. Landing too fast, using too much runway, and not appreciating the thrust lag had almost resulted in Ken going off the end of the runway. Despite Ken pushing the Meteor's thrust levers forward when he had realised he had botched his approach, the two-or three-second lag before his engines finally spooled up and delivered some thrust to power the Meteor into a climb, nearly saw him crash.

It was a bad case of complacency over one's own ability, John decided as he noted Ken's attitude.

'The programme's going well,' Wing Commander Hill told the pilots at a meeting some six months after they had begun Meteor operations at West Raynham. 'I can also tell you that Command is very pleased with the additional tactical insights and methods being recognised and developed for the aircraft here at CFE. Good work, gentlemen.'

They all smiled at that compliment.

'We have probably taken our development flying as far as possible at present,' John said. 'There are several things we still need to do, but not much, so when do we start developing our display routines?'

'Glad you asked that, Squadron Leader. All three of you can take some leave when we reach current development programme end, and after you get back from your leave we will move into working up some demonstration flying. Meantime, keep up the good work, and get safely through the last few items on the programme.'

'I wonder how the Meteors will be used in the longer term,' Jack said as they walked back to their operational area, where the two Meteor IIIs they were using sat waiting.

'I think we are seeing the beginning of the end of piston fighters,' John responded.

'I think we may be asked to use them soon in some secret missions,' Ken interjected.

'What would they be?' John asked.

'I think there's a possibility we will be tasked with offensive ops in the jet.'

'Offensive ops? Against whom? Germany has already surrendered.'

'The Japanese,' Ken said. 'They will fight on. They don't know the concept of surrender. It will require something special to end it with them. I reckon we might find a couple of squadrons of Meteors will be sent to that theatre.'

Absolute rubbish, thought John, but he simply said, 'Oh, I doubt it, but we'll see.'

Jack, who had been watching on, pulled a face at John, signalling that he agreed Ken was well off the mark.

'What a glorious day,' John proclaimed as he and Jack met outside the briefing room at West Raynham. It was the height of summer in England, and the war in Europe had ended two months previously. The pilots on the special jet programme at the Central Fighter Establishment had finished their Meteor development flying and were just back from a short leave.

'Indeed. I think the gods are celebrating the end of the war in Europe, along with everyone else, and brightening up the weather for us.' Jack replied with a grin.

'How are you two?' Ken called as he rounded the corner of the building and saw John talking to Jack.

'Fine, thanks, Ken. Refreshed and ready to go with whatever is next,' John responded.

'Let's go in and see what's planned,' Jack suggested.

Wing Commander Hill was already in the briefing room, and with him was a bespectacled, middle-aged man. He was a civilian, John judged from the suit he was wearing and the bowler hat he carried, together with his small leather briefcase.

'Gentlemen, welcome back. I trust you had a well-earned break and you're now ready for your next task.' Without waiting for any response, he continued, gesturing towards his visitor. 'May I introduce you to Mr Edward Symons, from the Ministry of Trade and Export?'

Hands were shaken as the gentleman from the Ministry was welcomed.

'He wants to talk to you about next steps with the Meteor.' He waved towards his guest, inviting him to begin.

'For some months I have been working with Air Ministry regarding the new Meteor jet aircraft, an aircraft with which I understand you three gentlemen are very familiar.'

They all smiled their agreement.

'The government is very keen to take an early lead in the use of jet fighters, by both ourselves and our allies. The Meteor has represented good progress in technology and propulsion systems, and we want to get our aircraft established with other countries as soon as we can. That means taking a lead in aeronautical development and marketing the aircraft to Britain's commercial advantage. Belgium, France, and Turkey have all expressed an interest in looking at the Meteor as they rebuild their air forces following the cessation of hostilities.'

'Japan is still engaging the West,' Ken interjected. 'Would Meteors be something that may assist in that theatre?'

'That is not something being considered,' Symons replied, clearly taken aback by the question.

'Oh, I thought it would help clinch our air superiority as Allied forces get closer to Japan, and ensure an early end to hostilities there,' Ken persevered.

Wing Commander Hill, clearly embarrassed by the interruption and foolish idea, made it quite clear he considered the suggestion had little merit. 'I think, Squadron Leader Smiley, deployment of the Meteor to the Asian theatre is highly unlikely. The US Air Force has already achieved control in the air over Japan. Nor is it a practical proposal for Meteors to be involved in that theatre. Getting our jets over there, even if they were wanted, would require shipping capacity not currently available, and we don't have sufficient aircraft available to send in any event. Nor do we have enough operationally ready pilots to fly them.'

'It's unnecessary for another reason as well,' Symons added. 'I can't go into detail, but the Americans expect to be in a position to bring the war against the Japanese to an end very quickly, sometime in the next few weeks.'

Ken gave an exaggerated shrug of his shoulders, as if to suggest he was not convinced his idea should not at least be considered. Everybody ignored him and focused on what Symons went on to say.

'Because of the interest being shown by other countries, we have decided to send the Meteors on a demonstration tour in the coming months. We want our allies to see the value in operating and acquiring fighter jets — British-built fighter jets.'

Symons went on for another twenty minutes, outlining the importance the government placed on a demonstration tour being successful, and being able to convince various friendly countries of the value in acquiring jets. But they had to be British jets. He warned the pilots that the Americans were also trying to get commitments from other air forces to buy their new fighter jet, something called a Shooting Star.

After Symons had left, Hill spoke to the three pilots.

'The plan is to show the Meteor in Belgium first, then France. Turkey's interest will have to wait until their people involved are going to be somewhere closer to Britain. We aren't attempting any long-distance deployments. Western Europe will be as far as we go.

'I want you to work up a display routine for the Meteors. It should demonstrate minimum take-off and landing distances, rate of climb from sea-level, and some high-speed passes. Also include low-level handling and some aerobatic manoeuvres. I'm thinking barrel-rolls and loops, but I'll leave it to you chaps at the end of the day. You are the active pilots in the machine. Let me know what you plan; I will authorise it after discussion with you if it looks okay. Then you will need to go away and practise it, a lot. You will be demonstrating to an expert audience. I want performances that leave them impressed, but to be clear, gentlemen, that isn't a licence to push the safety envelope to an unacceptable level. A flying incident would be a poor outcome and would certainly not win CFE any points with top brass.'

'Of course, sir,' John replied. 'We understand what's needed. A demo to impress, but not by taking any undue risk. We can achieve a fine balance.'

Over the next six weeks, John, Jack, and Ken worked up a display that would show the Meteor to best advantage. To guard against any unforeseen mechanical issues causing a temporary grounding, it was decided that both the Meteors they flew would go on any demonstration trip. Then they would have a spare aircraft available to fly the display, if that became necessary. Similarly, all three pilots would go, taking turns to fly exhibitions and providing cover should there be any issue affecting someone's fitness to fly.

Not long after the pilots had perfected their display, Wing Commander Hill called a meeting with them in his office.

'Right, we have a demonstration request,' he said. 'The Chief of the Turkish General Staff is visiting Tangmere on Saturday next week. He is due to arrive at the station at eleven-thirty that day, and will inspect a static display of aircraft, including a Meteor. Then, after looking at the workings of the local ground-controlled approach unit, he will move to the control tower to observe a flying display. That's where you come in, to show the Meteor.'

'Are we supplying the static display Meteor as well, sir?' John asked.

'Yes, we are. I suggest you position down there two or perhaps three days prior, to get set up. The adjutant will coordinate your logistics. Squadron Leader Noble, you are OC on this expedition. Thank you.'

It was a busy few days for John, as he liaised with the adjutant and signed off on the various arrangements being put in place. He decided he and Jack would each take a Meteor down to Tangmere. Ken would travel in the transport bringing ground crew and baggage.

When John and Jack landed at Tangmere to begin preparations, Ken was already there. The ground crew had arrived earlier that day to begin setting up in the hangar allocated to them and their two Meteors.

The day of the display dawned fine, with little wind. John was pre-flighting his aircraft when someone who had come up behind him suddenly spoke. John had not heard them approaching and whirled around in surprise. It was Edward Symons, from the Ministry of Trade and Export.

'Hello, Squadron Leader Noble. Nice to see you again. You all ready to impress the Turkish delegation?'

'Oh, hello. Didn't hear you coming. Yes, we have a routine ready that will show the Meteor very well, we think.'

'Great. This is important. We are relying on you to put on an unforgettable display for our visitors. Can you outline your routine to me?'

'I'm a bit pushed at present. I want to be ready at the specified time, but I can give you a moment. Normal take-off, followed by a rate-of-climb demonstration. Then a low-level handling display. After that, two high-speed passes, one inverted. That's about it.'

'How low will you be when you fly your high-speed passes?'

'I will see how it goes in the air, but the plan is not to go below three hundred feet.'

'The Turkish delegation will be watching from the tower cab. It would be impressive if you went past at a height that required them to look down on your aircraft in flight, as it goes past.'

'That would require me to be less than one hundred feet above the ground. That won't be happening.'

'Come on, man!' Symons virtually shouted. 'We need to impress.'

John looked at him coldly. 'I make the decisions about what is done and not done in the aircraft. I will not be descending below three hundred feet above ground level during the display itself.'

'I clearly need to talk to someone further up the ladder than you. Good day, Squadron Leader,' he responded as he stomped off.

The day after the display, Wing Commander Hill sat down

with the pilots to discuss how it had gone. 'I hear the Turkish delegation thought the Meteor a very capable and impressive aeroplane, so well done, chaps,' he said.

Edward Symons has clearly not taken up his complaint about me not flying as low as he wanted, with the wing commander, John decided.

'We have another demonstration request,' Hill went on. 'This time in France, Le Bourget, on the twenty-ninth. Just repeat what you did at Tangmere. That was well-received.'

Three weeks later, the Meteor demonstration team was in France. They had been there for two days and were ready to display the following morning. John and Jack were in the hangar, discussing the manoeuvres they planned to fly during the demonstration. It would be the same as at Tangmere, they had decided, but Jack was to fly on this occasion.

'We need to talk,' Ken said as he came in.

'What's the issue?' John asked, noting that Ken seemed agitated.

'The hangar next door has its main doors shut. When I was scooting around to get my bearings in the operational area, I stuck my head through one of the side-doors. The Yanks are here, with a Lockheed Shooting Star. I saw it parked in there. We aren't the only ones demonstrating a jet fighter to the French.'

'And the Belgians,' John added. 'I was advised by Wing Commander Hill as we were about to depart that he had just learnt that the Belgium Air Force would be sending observers as well.'

'Is this a fly-off between two potential suppliers of jet fighters?' Jack queried.

'I think it's more likely the French and Belgians simply thought there would be value in looking at both jets, seeing as they have gathered for an evaluation any way. It's not a head-to-head,' John replied confidently.

'You Limeys the people flying Friday?' an American voice asked them from the doorway.

They all looked around. A smiling leather-jacketed man stood there. From the insignia and decals on his jacket, he was obviously United States Army Air Force. John was the first to respond, stepping towards the visitor with his hand outstretched.

'We are. I'm Squadron Leader John Noble,' he said, as his hand was gripped so firmly it almost hurt. 'The gentlemen with me are Squadron Leaders Piper and Smiley.'

'Well, I'm mighty pleased to meet y'all. I'm flying the P-80 on demonstration, immediately before you guys fly your routine. What you got planned?'

'We are still working through that detail, but a basic handling display, really,' John responded.

'Ah well, I will leave you to your prep. Just popped in to say hello. May see you in the accommodation this evening. So long.'

John turned to Jack and Ken after the American had left. 'Competition was always going to be a factor,' he said. 'The Americans are chasing the same sales as Mr Symons from the Ministry, although I hadn't expected them to be here today. Anyway, it shouldn't change anything. We have our routine planned. You are flying it, Jack, so just carry on as normal. I know I don't need to say this, but we stick to the rehearsed plan. No special effort outside that, with some special endeavour designed to impress. We fly precisely as planned with no spur-of-the-moment variations. That's when mistakes get made.'

'I've got that. I'm not going to do anything silly trying to ensure we impress people more than the Americans might.'

'I think we should try something a little more spectacular,' Ken argued. 'Just going down the runway lower than our three-hundred foot minimum would add some excitement to our display. Surely we could add something like that?'

'No. We keep to our programme, as planned. We are not varying anything because the Americans are here demonstrating their jet as well,' John replied.

The next morning, right on time at eleven hundred hours, there was the roar of a jet engine from the direction of the runway. John and Ken, who were both in the control tower to observe the US jet display — and Jack's display, which would begin immediately after that first demonstration — both looked towards the far end of the runway. The American P-80 Shooting Star was in its take-off roll.

It went straight into its routine on becoming airborne. First it entered a steep turn to the right at about four hundred feet above the ground. That turn took it directly over the tower's outdoor observation platform, at low level. Impressive for the observers standing there. Then it rolled wings-level, crossing the tower, and what John thought must have been full power was applied. The Shooting Star rocketed up into a rapid climb of several thousand feet. At the top of its ascent, with its airspeed reducing fast, it pitched nose-down and entered a descending spiral dive, levelling at what John guessed was two hundred feet. It then flashed back over the tower, heading towards the runway. On reaching the runway, it rolled hard left and flew parallel to it.

On its pass over the tower, the Shooting Star had pulled up into a steep climb at the very last moment. *Impressive, no doubt about that,* John thought, *but risky. The late pull-up was exciting, but a misjudgement would have had the French and Belgian top brass wiped out. Just as well he got it right.*

As John continued watching the American aircraft, it reached the aerodrome boundary and entered a steep turn back, to follow the runway again. Once established above the runway, the jet rolled inverted and descended closer to the surface. *Christ,* thought John, *he's down to fifty feet, if that, inverted!*

As he watched, the Shooting Star rose two or three hundred feet, rolled through three hundred and sixty degrees, and then eased back down close to the runway surface again, still inverted. Then the American pilot repeated the manoeuvre, but this time, on completing his roll back to inverted, he pushed forward on his control stick to take him into a vertical climb. *Uncomfortable negative G-load there,* John thought. The Shooting Star was three seconds into that climb, passing through what John guessed was about eight hundred feet, when there was a flash of flame from the jet's tailpipe, and it lost thrust. At that height and in that position, there was no chance the aircraft could be recovered by the pilot as it literally fell from the sky. It exploded in a ball of fire in front of the horrified onlookers on the tower's observation platform. Even at the distance involved, they could feel the heat.

Back at RAF West Raynham two days later, John, Jack, and Ken were discussing the display accident with Wing Commander Hill. The remainder of the demonstration day at Le Bourget had been cancelled after the crash of the Shooting Star, and they had packed up and returned to England as soon as they could. Everybody was affected by the accident.

'I saw what happened,' John said, 'as did Ken. Jack was in our aircraft, preparing, so he only saw the aftermath.'

'Whatever caused the crash, it's a bad show for jet fighters,' Hill said.

'Yes,' said John, 'it was a high-risk display, and unfortunately it went wrong and the pilot paid the price. Boundaries were pushed when he rolled inverted to inverted, down the runway at very low level, but it was the negative-gee push into a vertical climb from ground level that surprised me. I think that may have contributed to a compressor stall. The enquiry will no doubt find out why the engine lost power, but whatever the reason, there was no way the pilot could recover the aircraft from that position. That's the reason manoeuvring like that close to the ground is usually avoided.'

'I hope something I said to the pilot didn't contribute,' Ken suddenly said.

They all looked at him enquiringly.

'I told him on the evening before the display that we had worked up a new and daring routine that would impress watchers, with low-level inverted passes, and bunting from that into a vertical climb from ground level. I was just trying to make him feel he would have a problem displaying against our aircraft. He laughed and said all that meant was that he would just have to match us.'

'The bunt from inverted is exactly what he did in the lead-up to the crash,' John said, feeling shocked. 'Has he taken what you said as gospel, and tried to do something difficult and unrehearsed? Surely not.'

'Okay, gentlemen, stop there,' Hill intervened. 'The US pilot was a skilled operator, and he made his own decisions. He was caught out by an engine malfunction, Squadron Leader Smiley. What you said to him is not anything like a contributory cause, so let's not even go there.'

'It probably does highlight the pressures associated with competition between Britain and the US, though, sir,' John said.

'Yes, there's no doubt about how the stakes are seen at senior levels,' Jack added. 'Just before my scheduled take-off time for the Meteor demo at Le Bourget, Edward Symons from the Ministry dropped by the hangar to give me a message he described as "coming from the top." I was to fly in a way that would be impressive and memorable, and if that involved me going outside the parameters agreed with my OC, that was okay with those who mattered.'

'Damn him — he tried that with me at Tangmere too. He got grumpy when I said it would not be happening,' John said, fuming.

'All right, gentlemen, I understand the issues around demonstration flights,' said Hill. 'I don't agree with what appears to be coming down the chain, and we'll stick to what we have planned for our demonstrations. The P-80 accident at Le Bourget may be an example of what succumbing to commercial pressure can bring, but we won't talk about that outside this room. You can be assured I will follow up on the suggestions that appear to be being made that we should not be concerned about taking inappropriate risks to make our demonstrations impressive.'

Wing Commander Hill was looking grim, John thought, as he, Jack, and Ken met with him in his office two weeks later.

'I have heard back from Command regarding our demonstration of the Meteor. Everyone there who is involved in the jet programme considers the operational parameters for Meteor flight demonstrations are for you, as the pilots flying, and for me, as your Commanding Officer, to establish.'

'That's good to hear, sir,' John responded.

'But that's not all. Sorry.'

The pilots all looked expectantly at Hill. What else did he have for them?

'Whitehall has also become involved in this particular issue, and the politicians seem to be adopting a different position.'

John's heart sank. What did the politicians want? And what did they even know about flying?

Hill then spelt out the message from Whitehall. It was unwelcome. The politicians — supported by several senior bureaucrats who wanted to ensure they were seen to be supportive of their masters — had made it clear they considered that taking "measured" risks was necessary to impress and gain sales.

'We can put on a damn good show without taking undue risks,' John argued.

Hill spread his arms to show his exasperation. 'I agree with you,' he said, 'and I can tell you that RAF Command pushed back, repeating that the pilots operating the aircraft were the people who should be making the decisions affecting safety in Meteor demonstrations. That was thought to be the end of the matter, but a few days ago the bureaucrats responded with a completely new operating model. They said that it had been decided to split developmental flying and demonstration flying. Developmental flying of jets would remain with the Central Fighter Establishment, but demonstration flights to help market British jet fighters would fall to a new state organisation, yet to be named, but charged with managing Britain's aviation sales push. Each of you will be effectively working for this new government entity, as demonstration pilots seconded by the RAF.'

'That takes RAF Command out of the loop for the detail of demonstration flights, then?' John asked.

'Correct. You will be answerable to the management of the new organisation, not Fighter Command.'

John saw immediately what the government officials were trying to do. 'So, we may be exposed to undue demonstration demands, and we will have no redress to Command if we think there is an operational issue? We are effectively employees being given an instruction by our managers, who will be government servants with a jet aircraft sales agenda?'

'I'm afraid so,' Hill responded. 'I know it is far from satisfactory from your perspectives as pilots, but it's the government's response to ensure they get what they want. There's not much the RAF will be able to do regarding any jet demonstration operations you are asked to fly. You will be subject to your employer's instruction, and no longer be flying under the Service's operational purview.'

'Do we know who will be in charge?' John snapped, none too happy with what he was hearing.

'I understand that Edward Symons has been appointed manager.'

That is ridiculous, John thought. He was thinking of Symons' actions regarding their demonstration flights to date.

'I think that's likely to be counterproductive so far as a successful sales campaign is concerned. An incident will kill interest very quickly, as we saw following Le Bourget. Restructuring management and control to get around aviation safety protocols is just wrong, and high risk,' John said.

Hill nodded. 'I agree with you. It's difficult, but that's what the government wants, so they have taken it out of our hands.'

Thinking about what had been said, later that day, John

reached a conclusion. He decided that he did not want to be involved with and controlled by politicians and bureaucrats who knew little about aviation safety who were prepared to go to the trouble of undertaking a restructuring exercise so that they could direct how Meteor demonstrations would be undertaken. It was short-sighted, and probably dangerous. *Damn, I might just resign, return to New Zealand, and rejoin Dad on the farm,* he thought. *I'm not needed here now the war's over. Lots of pilots are being released from the Service, at present, I will just be one more of them.*

A week later, after some more consideration, John decided that he would resign his commission. He wanted nothing to do with the jet demonstration proposals being pushed by the politicians and bureaucrats.

'I plan to return to my family's farm in New Zealand, now that the war has ended,' he gave as his reason for resigning. He had decided not to share with the RAF that he found the approach of some of those involved in the British government's attempt to achieve commercial aviation sales success, unacceptable.

John travelled back to New Zealand as quickly as possible and was greeted by his delighted parents.

'It's so good to see you back, John,' his mother said as they stood in the familiar homestead kitchen on the Noble family farm.

'I'm very happy to be here,' John replied, giving her a hug, 'and it's good to see the property looking in good heart.'

'Could you do a stock round for me, John?' his father smiled. 'I know you want to look over the place.'

'I do. I'll go now.' John was looking forward to a wander around the farm in the sunshine.

232

As he walked across the field adjacent to the slow-flowing Clutha River, he mused about the day, nearly eight years ago, when a small aircraft had flown over him here, and the pilot had waved. That had sent John off on his aviation quest.

Since then, he had learnt to fly, operated the best fighter aircraft the world had to offer, and seen service in several different war theatres. He was happy to have survived, but he was conscious that many had not. Fellow pilots who were friends had died in the conflicts. He paused as he thought about Mary, struggling to fight back an all-consuming wave of melancholy.

The harsh sound of an aircraft's fast-turning propellor pulled John back to the present. Looking up, he saw there was an air force Harvard flying over the farm. *It will be a cross-country exercise from RNZAF Taieri to Invercargill, by the look of his track*, he decided. *Maybe some young man will look up at that aircraft as it passes overhead, and be inspired to take up flying.* He knew there was little to match the feeling a pilot had when slicing through the sky, watching the world pass by below.

With those thoughts, Squadron Leader John Noble, DFC, RAF (retired), turned to walk back to his family's homestead. There was a wide smile on his face. Now he was home again, enjoying the peace and quiet of the countryside, and memories of war were pushed out of his mind. It was time for a new life.

A NOTE TO THE READER

Dear Reader,

I hope you enjoyed *Despair and Triumph*, the third and final novel in the *John Noble Fighter Ace Thriller* series. While the books in the series are works of fiction, the stories they tell are inspired by real people and actual events. As this book is the last in the series, I will now share with you that the career path of the central character, John Noble, is based on that taken by a New Zealander during World War Two, Squadron Leader John Noble Mackenzie, DFC.

After leaving his family farm in South Otago, New Zealand, to take up a flying role with the RAF, Squadron Leader Mackenzie joined a Spitfire squadron and flew in defence of the troops at Dunkirk. After Dunkirk, he was engaged in the Battle of Britain — earning a DFC presented to him at Buckingham Palace by King George. Then he was posted to Singapore, where he flew against the Japanese. After the fall of Singapore, he managed to escape back to New Zealand, where he helped the RNZAF prepare its pilots for the aerial warfare they would soon face in the Pacific. Back in the European theatre after his time in New Zealand, Squadron Leader Mackenzie led his Spitfire squadron over the Normandy Beaches on D-Day, and post-war, he flew as an RAF demonstration pilot in the Gloster Meteor.

Some of the operations described in the books were taken from Mackenzie's logbook — including his trans-Africa flight in a Hurricane, but without the forced landing. The clashes and concerns with the RAF hierarchy that my character, John Noble, has are purely fiction, and neither did he resign because of bureaucratic interference in his Meteor demonstration flights.

Another fact that I want to share with you is that Squadron Leader John Noble Mackenzie, DFC, was my father. I have been pleased to write the *John Noble Fighter Ace Thriller* series as a partially fictionalised account of my father's wartime career.

After retiring from the RAF at the end of 1957, my father returned to New Zealand, but he did not go back to farming. Instead, he acquired the Ford Dealership for South Otago and successfully ran a business there for some years. He died in 1993.

Thank you for taking the time to read *Despair and Triumph*. If you would like to rate this book on **Amazon** or **Goodreads**, or leave a review, that would be appreciated. Readers are welcome to get in touch with me via my **Facebook Author Profile** at **"David Mackenzie NZ writer"**.

Kind regards

David Mackenzie

Sapere Books is an exciting new publisher of brilliant fiction and popular history.

To find out more about our latest releases and our monthly bargain books visit our website: **saperebooks.com**